SHERLOCK JONES

THE WILLOUGHBY BANK ROBBERY

Other Books by Ed Dunlop

The Young Refugee Series
Escape to Liechtenstein
The Search for the Silver Eagle
The Incredible Rescues

Sherlock Jones, Junior Detective
Sherlock Jones: The Assassination Plot
Sherlock Jones: The Willoughby Bank Robbery

SHERLOCK JONES

THE WILLOUGHBY BANK ROBBERY

ED DUNLOP

JOURNEY
FORTH™

Greenville, South Carolina

Library of Congress Cataloging-in-Publication Data

Dunlop, Ed, 1955-

Sherlock Jones : the Willoughby Bank robbery / by Ed Dunlop.

p. cm.

Summary: Seventh-graders Jasper "Sherlock" Jones and Penny Gordon again put their Christian beliefs into action when they witness a bank robbery and set out to find the thieves and clear the name of a friend.

ISBN 1-59166-314-8 (perfect bound pbk. : alk. paper)

[1. Bank robberies—Fiction. 2. Christian life—Fiction. 3. Gossip—Fiction. 4. Mystery and detective stories.] I. Title.

PZ7.D92135Sh 2004

[Fic]—dc22

2004020921

Design by Craig Oesterling

Cover illustration by Scott Freeman

Composition by Melissa Matos

© 2005 BJU Press

Greenville, SC 29614

Printed in the United States of America

ISBN 1-59166-315-6

15 14 13 12 11 10 9 8 7 6 5 4 3 2 1

3-2-20

Dedicated to the Parker kids

*"Whether therefore
ye eat, or drink,
or whatsoever ye do,
do all to the glory of God."*

I Corinthians 10:31

CONTENTS

ONE

IT HAPPENED IN WILLOUGHBY!

Willoughby is a dreary little town; nothing exciting ever happens. Living here is about as much fun as doing the dishes after Thanksgiving dinner. I should know. I've lived here all my life. But one memorable day in June, we got all the excitement we could handle. The sleepy little town of Willoughby could not have been more surprised if a UFO had landed in the middle of Main Street and little green men had started passing out samples of Martian cuisine.

It happened on a boring Monday afternoon. School was out for the summer. Sherlock and I were walking down Main Street, heading for the First National Bank of Willoughby to deposit the four dollars I had gotten for baby-sitting the Spriggs twins.

Sherlock was sauntering along with his head down, trying to negotiate a little steel ball bearing through a wooden maze. I had the box that the maze had come in and was trying to read it as we walked along.

"The future of this planet depends on us!" the package proclaimed in bright green letters. "Listen to this," I said to Sherlock, reading the box to him. "This product made from reforested trees. Package made from 100% recycled materials. Instructions printed in recycled English."

I elbowed him to get his attention, and he glanced up from the game. "Does it really say that, Penny?"

"Well, not the last part," I admitted. "I made that up. But this recycling thing is getting out of hand. Next thing you know, they'll be recycling toothpaste and . . . and facial tissues!"

I glanced over at Sherlock, but he had already gone back to the maze.

"Sherlock, look out!" I called suddenly, but it was too late. Head down, attention focused totally on the game in his hands, he had walked smack into a lady standing in the middle of the sidewalk.

That's Sherlock for you. When something has his attention, everything else around him is totally forgotten. "The power of total concentration," he calls it. If that's what it is, believe me, he has it.

The impact of the collision knocked the maze from his skinny hands, and he looked up, slightly startled, and nearly as embarrassed as a sheep after springtime shearing. The woman he had bumped was rather large—that's a polite way of putting it—and apparently was a tourist. She had an expensive camera on a strap around her neck and was wearing a rather large pair of fluorescent pink shorts. Some people just do not look good in shorts, and let me tell you, she was one of them.

The woman had been preparing to snap a picture of one of the crumbling old buildings on Main Street when Sherlock bumped her. The impact had knocked the camera from her grasp. Fortunately the strap had saved the camera from a tragic end, and the instrument was swinging from the end of its leash like the pendulum on some strangely overweight grandfather clock.

"I'm sorry, ma'am," my friend stammered. "I didn't see you standing there!"

The woman threw back her round head and bellowed with laughter. Her chubby cheeks swelled outward as she laughed, giving her face the appearance of a stuffed doll.

"How about that, Harold?" she boomed to a timid-looking man in Bermuda shorts standing nervously nearby. "He didn't see me!" She laughed again. "He said he didn't see me."

Wiping the tears of laughter from her pudgy eyes, she turned her attention back to Sherlock. "Son, it's been a long time since anyone's had a hard time seeing me!"

Sherlock nervously repeated his apologies, and we hurried on. I glanced back, and the woman was aiming her camera skyward again, chuckling to herself as she focused on the steeple of St. Jerome's Episcopal Church.

A long black Lincoln slowly floated past us. A thin little white-gloved hand fluttered in Sherlock's direction. The driver was Mrs. Peabody, probably the richest lady in the whole state. She must be about eighty. She pilots her big automobile around town from her perch atop two pillows placed on the driver's seat. She never goes over fifteen miles an hour, so I guess she doesn't pose too much of a threat to the other drivers of Willoughby.

"There's Mrs. Peabody," I said, elbowing Sherlock in the ribs.

He glanced up, slightly irritated at being interrupted again. "Huh?" Then he saw the Lincoln. "Oh." He waved, and the huge car continued noiselessly down the street.

We reached the bank, one of the oldest structures in Willoughby. The front of the building makes you think of a fort or a castle. It's built of dull gray cement, and long green stains mark the walls. Up close to the roof, just under the bronze rain gutters, stone figures of lions and angels stand guard. It must have been a beautiful building when it was first built, but now it just looks old. Sherlock says the bank looks as if George Washington's great-grandfather had built it.

When you go inside the bank, your footsteps echo on the polished wooden floor with a hollow, spooky sound. The tellers stand behind little windows with little bars in front of them. You get the idea that they're keeping your money in some sort of jail.

But our bank does have some modern stuff. Two years ago, they installed a new stainless steel vault, as well as electronic alarms and a security camera. I hope my money's safe. I have thirty-seven dollars in my account, and I'll have forty-one in just a few minutes. Sherlock has over five hundred dollars in the bank.

Just a few steps from the door, Sherlock stopped and turned toward the street. I stopped too and looked up at the sign on the bank door. Six-inch letters molded into the cement spelled out "The First National Bank of Willoughby," but somebody had taken black paint and crossed out the word "First." Above it, they had written "Only." It was done years ago as a Halloween prank, but the bank management never had it sandblasted off. My mom says that it has been there since she was a girl.

A voice behind me boomed, "What a quaint little town! Such a charming little village!"

I glanced over my shoulder, and it was the lady tourist again, still flourishing her camera. Her husband held her purse while she took a shot of the bank. Her accent told me that she's not from anywhere around Willoughby. I think she's probably from England. I still hadn't heard her husband say anything.

Sherlock nudged me just then and pointed toward the street. An old green car with the engine running was parked directly in front of the bank. "It's a getaway car," he whispered, his eyes shining with excitement. "Penny, there's a bank robbery in progress!"

I gave him a scornful look. "Don't be ridiculous," I chided. "You've been reading too many detective stories."

"I don't read detective stories, Penny."

He stepped to the rear of the car for a look at the license plate, and I stood on the sidewalk, hands on my hips, doing my best to look disgusted with him. I saw him glance up toward me with a huge grin on his face, and suddenly the grin changed to a look of horror.

Sherlock dashed toward me, grabbed me, and shoved me against the wall of the bank—hard. I hit the cement wall beside the door so violently that I was sure some ribs were broken. I had never seen Sherlock move so fast.

I flared in anger. "What are you—"

Just then, the heavy glass doors of the bank flew open, and two men came dashing out. One had a long gun in his hands (a shotgun, I think), and the other had a revolver with a long, long barrel. Both men had scraggly, black beards, and both were carrying big white canvas bank bags.

As they dashed for the waiting car, the man with the shotgun spotted Sherlock and me. He started to turn toward us with his weapon, hesitated for an instant, and then turned and sprinted to the car.

The other man had run around to the driver's side of the vehicle. They both opened the doors at the same instant. With lightning-quick movements, they hurled the bank bags to the floor of the car and jumped in, slamming the doors after them.

I was weak with astonishment and fear. Legs trembling, I sank to the sidewalk. My heart was pounding as if it wanted out of my rib cage. My entire body seemed to turn to jelly. I was so scared I could hardly move.

But the big tourist lady with the camera cried out in delight. She sprang into the street, moving with speed and agility that was amazing for someone her size. She raised her camera, and as the driver slammed the car into gear, she snapped a picture of the rear of the vehicle.

"Isn't this exciting, Harold?" she called. "This is a real live bank robbery!" She raised her camera and snapped again, but the getaway car was nearly out of sight.

The woman then turned and clicked off another shot of the bank, a grin of delight spread across her broad face. "I can't wait to get home and show Mildred these shots," she chortled to her husband. "Wait till I tell her what happened! When she sees . . ."

The big woman stopped in midsentence. Her mouth was open like a puffer fish. She gave a little cry and then bustled forward. Harold had fainted.

Down on my knees on the sidewalk, I felt like joining him. Sherlock and I had just witnessed a bank robbery—right here in Willoughby!

TWO

THE WITNESSES

I suppose I ought to introduce Sherlock and myself. I'm Penelope Gordon, but everyone calls me Penny. I'm twelve years old, and I just finished sixth grade about a week ago. My mom probably would want me to let you know that I was on the B honor roll this year. I like school—at least most of the time.

I'm pretty tall for a seventh-grader, and I'm thin, with long blond hair that can be an absolute nightmare to do anything with. My dad says that I have more freckles per square inch than a coot's egg. I'm not bad looking, but I'll never win a Miss Universe contest either. However, I can throw a softball farther than most of the boys in my class can hit one. My dad says I'm a tomboy. I guess that's really all you need to know about me.

My friend Sherlock is really named Jasper Jones, but he hates his given name. No one ever calls him by it anymore anyway, except maybe old Mrs. Peabody. When he uncovered the plot to assassinate the governor several months ago, a reporter from one of the big city newspapers compared him to the legendary detective Sherlock Holmes and the nickname stuck. Everybody calls him "Sherlock" now, even his mom and dad. Mr. and Mrs. Jones are OK, but why would anybody name a kid Jasper?

Sherlock is only eleven years old, but he skipped third grade, so he's in my class at school. He's a real brain. I mean, this guy is unreal. He has a photographic memory, which means that he can read a page, or even a whole book, and then tell you everything that he read word for word! You've never seen anything like it.

I remember one time this year when our class was reading aloud from our history books. Miss Wiggins noticed that Sherlock did not have his book open, so she asked him to stand and read next. To her astonishment, he stood and quoted the next page from memory! Like I said, this guy is unreal!

Just by looking at him, you'd never guess that he's one of the smartest people in the world. He's short and skinny, has dark, unruly hair that sticks up in the back, and wears thick glasses. The glasses make his eyes look about three times as big as they really are.

Sherlock runs his own detective agency from a little shed behind his house. A hand-lettered sign over the door proclaims "Sherlock Jones—Willoughby's Most Effective Detective." He keeps his records on a computer that he built from junk parts that the computer store threw away. He knows more about computers than most of the guys that work for Computer City.

Now don't get the idea that Sherlock's detective agency is just an eleven-year-old kid playing gumshoe. It's a real first-class detective agency, and he's solved some really tough cases. He started with cases at school—you know, stolen lunch money and stuff like that—and he's worked his way up to some really important ones. I guess I already told you that he uncovered a plot to kill the governor.

I guess I haven't told you much about Willoughby. I've lived here all my life, and so has Sherlock. We've known each other since we were little. Sherlock is my best friend, even if he is a boy.

Willoughby has a small green sign at the edge of town that says the population is 1,848. They need to change the sign though, because the Andersons moved to Oregon last week, and they have six kids.

Our town has three churches—Baptist, Methodist, and Episcopal—two grocery stores, and three filling stations. The entire Willoughby police force consists of three officers: the chief and two lieutenants. Our mayor pumps gas at Willis' Pump&Go station. As you can imagine, living in Willoughby is about as exciting as four hours of homework.

So anyway, that's why I was so amazed to see something as exciting as a bank robbery. I mean, right here in Willoughby!

I was kneeling on the sidewalk, the fat lady was bending over her unconscious husband, and Sherlock was writing down the license number of the getaway car on the back of his hand in green ink. He writes notes on the back of his hand all the time. I don't really know why he does it because he always remembers everything anyway.

He glanced up at the bank, then back to the empty curb where the car had been just moments before, and then wrote something else on his hand. I didn't see what he wrote.

A siren wailed just then, and a Willoughby police car came screaming up in front of the bank, lights flashing red and blue. The police station is just a block away.

Officer Bill jumped out and made his way through the crowd that was gathering in front of the bank. Officer Bill is a tall blond man with a friendly face and a pleasant smile. He's always nice to us kids. He's really good-looking, and he's not married.

The other Willoughby patrol car pulled up, and Chief Ramsey and Officer Clark climbed out. The chief is a short fat man with just a little fringe of hair around the sides of his head. He huffs and puffs when he walks, and the back of his light blue uniform shirt is always dark with sweat.

Lieutenant Clark is a tall man with dark hair, dark eyes, and a perpetual scowl on his face. Every time I see him, I get the idea that he's having a really bad day. He's the only one on the Willoughby police force that is scornful of Sherlock's detective work.

Another siren sounded, and the crowd moved back as a long, white ambulance pulled right up onto the sidewalk. The EMTs hurried a stretcher through the front doors of the bank, and it was then that we learned that Mr. Phillips, the elderly bank security guard, had been shot.

They brought him out on the stretcher just moments later. A transparent green oxygen mask was over his face, and his eyes were closed. His skin looked horribly pale, kind of bluish-white. I felt sorry for him and angry that the robbers would do a thing like that to a kind old man like Mr. Phillips. When I was little, he used to give me candy whenever my mom took me into the bank.

The stretcher was lifted into the ambulance. One of the EMTs climbed in beside it, and Chief Ramsey helped close the ambulance door. The siren wailed, and I prayed for Mr. Phillips as the vehicle sped out of town. General Hospital is twenty miles away.

Chief Ramsey hurried into the bank while the two officers took statements from the witnesses outside. The crowd pushed in close, each witness eager to give his or her version of the incident. The officers must have thought we were describing at least a dozen robberies. There were that many different accounts.

Officer Bill lifted his pen from his notepad and looked at the crowd of faces around him. "Can anyone give me a good description of the car?" he asked hopefully.

THE WITNESSES

"Green 1976 Chevy Impala," Sherlock responded immediately. "Four door, 400-cubic-inch engine with a badly worn right front tire, mud spattered across the entire rear end except the license plate, broken left tail light lens."

Officer Bill started writing, but an older man interrupted. "Hold it, Bill," he said, "this young man's description isn't quite accurate. I saw the car, and I was standing right there in front of the barbershop when it happened. The car was a dark color, but it wasn't green. Blue, maybe, or black. And I think it was a Mercury, about an '80."

"No, it was a Ford," a woman interjected. "I used to drive one just like it."

Sherlock turned and looked at me and shrugged his shoulders.

"Blue Mustang, Bill," a man's voice from the crowd insisted. "My kid had one that was identical, 'cept his was white."

A dozen voices clamored for Officer Bill's attention, each person certain that he or she could correctly identify the make and model of the getaway car. The problem was that no two witnesses could agree. One old lady even insisted that the bank robbers had been driving a red Volkswagen convertible!

An argument ensued between the blue Mustang man and a lady who was just sure that the getaway car was a black Mercedes.

"Mercedes?" the man growled. "Lady, you don't know your cars. If that was a Mercedes, I'm the emperor of China!"

"I was less than ten feet from the getaway car and I saw it clearly enough, sir," she retorted hotly. "It was most certainly a Mercedes!"

The man shook his head in disgust. "A Mustang doesn't even begin to look like a Mercedes." He snorted in derision. "Do you even know what a Mercedes looks like?"

"I guess I would know a Mercedes when I see one," the woman sniffed haughtily. "My family has owned a number of them."

To my surprise, the crowd began to take sides, even though some of the witnesses had to change their stories to do so. I noticed that most of the men were siding with the Mustang man, while the women seemed to agree that the car in question was a Mercedes. The argument grew louder and louder.

"Did anyone get the license number?" Officer Bill shouted, pen poised above the pad. The crowd fell silent for an instant.

"EJD 845," Sherlock answered.

"Hold it, Bill, he's wrong again," the older man said. "I saw it with my own eyes. The number was FOB 045. This young fellow's wearing glasses, and his eyesight's just not as keen as mine."

Sherlock sighed deeply.

Another witness spoke up. "The license number was EOD 008, Bill," she said. "It was plain as day."

A hand reached through the crowd just then and grabbed me by the arm, pulling me out of the mob. I turned. It was Sherlock. He had slipped around behind me. "Come on, let's get out of here," he muttered.

As we walked toward home, we discussed the robbery. "I can't believe this happened right here in Willoughby," I said. "Imagine! A bank robbery! In Willoughby, of all places!"

Sherlock nodded soberly. "I never would have suspected that it would happen here," he replied. I glanced at him in surprise. The way he said it, it almost seemed that he was disappointed with himself, as if he should have known in advance that the robbery was going to take place.

A sudden thought occurred just then. "You knew," I exclaimed. "When we first saw the car, you knew that a robbery was taking place! I laughed at you, but you were right! How did you know?"

He ducked his head as if he were embarrassed. "I didn't," he admitted sheepishly. "I guessed, which is something that I try to avoid. The green Chevy had all the earmarks of a getaway car, but I still should not have guessed before I had the facts."

"Who do you think the robbers were?" I asked. "Any ideas?"

He shook his head. "I'm not making any more foolish guesses, Penny. We'll have to wait until I have more facts to go on."

Just then two bicycles came flying past us and then did quick U-turns in the street as the riders recognized us. Tommy Moore and Nathan Galloway were our two class clowns, but today their facial expressions were serious. "You missed all the excitement," Tommy exclaimed, coasting slowly beside us. "The Willoughby bank was just robbed!"

"We were there," Sherlock replied quietly, but neither boy heard him.

"You won't believe what happened!" Nathan gushed excitedly. "Four guys on motorcycles roared up in front of the bank, shot out the front windows, and then rode right inside the bank!"

Sherlock groaned.

"They got away with more than a million dollars!"

"And this isn't the only bank robbery they're gonna do," Tommy told us proudly. His eyes flashed with excitement, and I could tell that he was enjoying the whole episode.

"Yeah, the robbers are planning to rob the bank in Spencerville tomorrow," Nathan cut in, "and maybe the one in Jackson after that!"

"How do you know all this?" Sherlock challenged.

Nathan snorted as if the question were an affront to his intelligence. "My cousin told me," he declared indignantly. "Her next door neighbor saw the whole thing."

"See you later," Tommy called, as both boys stood on their pedals and rushed off to spread the news.

Sherlock shook his head. "I knew this would happen. It's started already."

"What has?"

"The rumor mill. People who were not even present are telling others about what happened. There will be no end to the rumors that will fly in the next few days. And believe me, nothing good will come of it."

"Half of what they told us wasn't even true," I pointed out. "There weren't four bank robbers, and they weren't on motorcycles, and they didn't shoot out the bank windows—"

"And they probably aren't planning to rob the bank in Spencerville tomorrow," Sherlock finished, with a snort of disgust.

"Why do people make up stuff like this?" I asked of no one in particular. "The bank robbery was exciting enough just the way it happened. Why add details to the story that didn't even happen?"

"Gossip is like that," Sherlock reasoned. "When something like this happens, the story starts spreading from one person to another and before you know it, most of the truth has been replaced by misunderstandings or outright lies. And usually, someone ends up getting hurt as a result."

He shook his head. "No wonder the book of James says that the tongue is like a fire."

I remembered my friend the security guard. "Mr. Phillips didn't look very good. I hope he makes it!"

Sherlock nodded soberly. "So do I," he said. "We need to pray for him." He looked at his watch. "Penny, I'll come over after supper. We'll go over and discuss the robbery with Officer Bill."

I started down the gravel lane that leads to our house, then turned and waved to Sherlock. "See you tonight!"

He waved back.

The gravel crunched under my sneakers. I thrust my hand into the pocket of my culottes. My four dollars was still there, forgotten in the excitement of the Willoughby bank robbery.

THREE

THE ARREST

I heard a car approaching from behind, so I stepped to the side of the road to let it pass. The car slowed, and then stopped as it drew alongside. It was Gimpy Williams in his big old green Chevy.

Gimpy goes to our church and is one of the kindest men you'll ever meet. He was a drunkard for years and lost his family because of alcohol, but he got saved about three years ago. I've never seen anyone change as much as Gimpy did. I don't know his real name, but everyone in Willoughby calls him Gimpy. He got the nickname from the constant limp he has as a result of shrapnel he caught in the leg during the Vietnam War.

Gimpy lives about ten miles out of town in a little old farmhouse. It's about two or three miles closer for him to cut across the mountain on our lane than to take the highway around.

He poked his head out the window, that lazy grin of his slowly spreading across his rugged face. "Hi, Penny Loafer!" he called. "What's up?"

I mentioned the bank robbery, and to my surprise, he hadn't heard about it, so I told him the whole story. "Sherlock and I were going to the bank to deposit my baby-sitting money," I began, "and Sherlock noticed a car parked in front of the bank with the engine running. He told me that it was a getaway car, but I laughed at him. Two bank robbers came running out with guns just then, and if Sherlock hadn't pushed me against the wall of the bank, I don't know what would have happened. Both men got away with big sacks of money!"

"Nah," Gimpy said when I had finished. "You're making this up, Miss Penny!"

I shook my head. "You'll hear it on the news tonight," I answered. "Just wait and see."

He searched my face for some sign that I was teasing him and then decided I was serious. He frowned. "I can't believe that this would happen in Willoughby! I've been at my secret fishing hole most of the day, so I haven't even been into town. When did all this happen?"

"About an hour ago," I answered and then told him about Mr. Phillips being shot.

"No!" he exclaimed. His face darkened. "It makes you mad to think that anyone would shoot a kind old man like Phillips, doesn't it?"

"Pray for him, Gimpy," I said. "He didn't look very good when they took him away."

He nodded. "I will, Penny."

"Sherlock says that the bank robbers—"

"Gotta run, Penny," Gimpy interrupted me. He put the car in gear. "See you at church."

As his big green car pulled away, I thought to myself, "Gimpy's car looks a lot like the one the bank robbers had." I glanced at his license plate and then did a double take. I rubbed my eyes and looked again. "EJD 845," I read aloud. "Sherlock must have read the robbers' number wrong," I told myself. "That's Gimpy's license number!"

That evening, a knock on the door informed me of Sherlock's arrival. I quickly set the last stack of dishes in the cupboard, flipped the dishtowel over its hook on the end of the cabinet, and hurried from the kitchen. "See you later, Mom!" I called. "Sherlock and I are going over to Officer Bill's house!"

"Is your homework finished?" Mom wanted to know.

"School's out, remember?" I answered, as I headed out the door. "No homework till September!"

Sherlock was waiting on the porch. "Officer Bill's home," he told me. "His car's in the driveway."

Officer Bill lives next door, and in seconds, we were knocking on his door. He greeted us warmly. "Come in, come in," he invited. "I was just finishing supper. It's been quite a day! Care for a piece of cold pizza?"

We followed him into the kitchen. A big white flat pizza box lay on the table with three pieces of pepperoni pizza still there for the taking. It didn't even look good to me, but Sherlock started right in. He's always hungry.

"How much did the robbers get?" my detective friend asked with his mouth full of pizza.

The policeman sighed. "$180,000, all in cash," he replied. "These guys knew what they were doing. The Keepsafe armored truck had just made a delivery ten minutes before the robbery. They timed it perfectly."

"How is Mr. Phillips doing?" I asked.

Officer Bill shook his head slowly. "Not very well, I'm afraid. He's in critical condition at General. The bullet penetrated his left lung."

I sat down on the chair beside Sherlock, and Officer Bill tossed an envelope on the table between us. "Believe it or not, some woman got a snapshot of the getaway car," he said. "We got the license number, and everything!"

Sherlock nodded. "Mrs. Abernathy," he said. "She's from Vermont."

Officer Bill stared at him. "They had New York plates on their car," he asserted. "Why do you say she's from Vermont?"

"The car was a rental," Sherlock explained. "Big white Cadillac—this year's model. Bet they had a rough ride coming down here."

Officer Bill's mouth actually fell open. "You're right," he said. "That's the car! They asked me about a garage to have the car looked at. But that was after you left. How did you know that?"

"I noticed the wear pattern on the tires," Sherlock explained. "That car needs some front end work, bad! Apparently, the car rental agency didn't catch it, or they never would have sent it out like that. The Abernathys must not have done any high speed driving for the first part of their trip, or they would have noticed the problem right away."

"How do you know it's a rental car?" I asked.

"There was a small number on the back bumper," the young detective explained, "1218. That's a fleet number, so the car belongs to a large corporation or a rental agency. My guess is that it's a rental car, as even the large corporations would hardly have a fleet of over a thousand cars."

Officer Bill shook his head. "Sometimes you amaze me, Sherlock," he said. "How did you know their name, and that they were from Vermont?"

Sherlock grinned. "You don't expect me to divulge all my professional secrets, do you?" he laughed.

"Please, Sherlock," I begged. "I'll wonder about this for the rest of my life if you don't tell us!"

He laughed. "That part was easy," he admitted. "Mrs. Abernathy had her name and address on the outside of her camera bag."

Sherlock drew the pictures from the envelope, and we bumped heads as we both leaned forward to study them. He gripped the stack of photos in his left hand and used his right thumb to flip rapidly through the pictures. I leaned closer, trying to catch a glimpse of the photos. There were shots of the fire hall and the bakery, of the steeple of St. Jerome's, of the bank, of Harold Abernathy in front of the bank, and finally, the picture we were looking for.

"She takes good pictures," Sherlock commented. "Unusually good pictures."

Officer Bill nodded. "We couldn't have asked for better," he agreed.

He pulled that one photo from the rest and laid it on top, then set the entire stack on the table. I leaned over the photo, studying it along with Sherlock.

The picture clearly showed the back of the getaway car, license plate and all. The car was a green, 1976 Chevy Impala, just as Sherlock had described to Officer Bill. The robber in the passenger seat was visible through the back window of the car, the barrel of his shotgun sticking up above the back of the seat. The photo even showed the taillights clearly, and the left one was broken, just as Sherlock had said. How would anyone notice a detail like that, especially in the excitement of a bank robbery? But Sherlock had.

But what made me catch my breath was the license number of the car: EJD 845. That was the license plate number I had seen on Gimpy's old Chevy!

Officer Bill stuck a big forefinger toward the license plate in the photo. "Do you know whose tag number that is?" he asked.

Sherlock nodded. "Gimpy's," he said with a sigh.

We both stared at him. "How did you know that?" I asked.

He glanced at Officer Bill and then replied, "I can access a public DMV site on my computer. I checked this tag number as soon as I got home."

"What's 'DMV'?" I asked.

"Department of Motor Vehicles," Officer Bill answered. He shook his head again. "You amaze me, kid. But you're right. It's Gimpy's car. We arrested him just a little bit ago."

I jumped up from the table in shock. "Surely you don't think Gimpy did it!" I almost screamed. "He wouldn't rob a bank! He wouldn't! We've all seen the change in him since he got saved!"

Officer Bill nodded sadly. "There's more evidence than just this photo though, Penny. As you know, the bank had a security camera installed about two years ago. The robbery is on film."

"What did the camera show?" Sherlock asked.

"Well, one of the tellers was alert, and she managed to turn the camera on just a few seconds after the robbers came in the front door of the bank," Officer Bill answered, "so the camera recorded the entire robbery. I saw the film just before I left the station a little while ago. Two men came in, one armed with a shotgun, the other with a long-barreled revolver. Both men were average height, one slightly taller than the other one, and both had heavy beards. The camera shows them as they went back to the vault area, and then again as they came back out. But here's the clincher: the man with the revolver limped! I'm afraid it was Gimpy Williams."

I looked from Officer Bill to Sherlock. "But that can't be," I protested. "Gimpy didn't rob the bank!"

Officer Bill shrugged. "I didn't think so either," he replied. "But it's on the tape. And the snapshot of the license plate confirms it."

"Can we get a look at the film?" Sherlock asked.

Officer Bill ran a hand across his face before he answered. "I don't think the chief would allow it," he said finally. "That film is actually government property now. The FBI will be picking it up tomorrow."

"Wow," I said, "Will they be in on this?"

Officer Bill nodded. "Armed robbery is a federal offense."

Sherlock sat quietly, deep in thought.

"If they were to convict Gimpy," I queried, "how much time would he get?"

"We're looking at armed robbery and attempted murder," Officer Bill answered. "He'd get a minimum of twenty years, probably more."

Sherlock spoke up. "I've got to see that tape, Officer Bill."

But the big police officer shook his head. "Can't do it, pal. It's got to go to the FBI tomorrow."

"Couldn't you make a copy?" I asked.

"It's government property, Penny. I have to follow regulations."

"I've got to see that tape, Officer Bill. Please?" Sherlock was begging, and I could tell how much this meant to him.

Officer Bill laughed. "We already watched it five or six times at the station, Sherlock. There's nothing on it that I didn't tell you about. What's the big deal about seeing it?"

Sherlock sighed, and I could tell from his eyes that he was trying to decide how to word his next approach. "There are times when I . . ." He stopped, looked at me as if for support, and then began again. "There are times when I notice things that other people don't. There might . . . there might be things on the tape that you guys overlooked. If I could just view it one time . . ."

"Sorry, Sherlock. Chief Ramsey would never agree to that. I can't do it without his permission."

I plopped down on the couch beside Officer Bill. "Do you remember what Chief Ramsey said when Sherlock figured out the assassination plot and saved Governor Bradley's life?" I asked, feeling as if my input would be useless. But I had to try. "He told Sherlock that he would welcome his help the next time a difficult case came his way."

He smiled. "Chief was being polite, Penny." My face must have showed my feelings because he hastened to add, "Oh, he was impressed, Penny, and he was grateful for Sherlock's help. But—"

"But he didn't really mean it," I said glumly. "He was just being polite."

"Would Chief Ramsey grant permission for me to view the tape?" Sherlock asked.

Officer Bill thought for a moment and then finally threw up his hands in a gesture of surrender. "OK, you two, I'll tell you what I'll do. I'll call Chief Ramsey. If he says I can show it to you, I will. But if he says no, you can't hassle me. Fair enough?"

Sherlock nodded. "Fair enough."

Officer Bill walked into the kitchen and picked up the phone. Moments later we could hear him talking with Chief Ramsey, and he quickly explained what Sherlock wanted. We could only hear one side of the conversation, of course, but we could tell that Chief Ramsey wasn't thrilled with the idea.

"But Chief—" Officer Bill walked back into the room, holding the phone to his ear and listening. "Yes, sir, but—" The look on his face told us that the news wasn't good.

I glanced at Sherlock, and then laughed at the expression on his thin face. He was leaning forward intently, listening to Officer Bill's side of the conversation, and looking as if the next few seconds would determine whether he lived or died. I've never seen such a look of anticipation.

"But think about what happened when Governor Bradley came to Willoughby," the young officer argued. "If it hadn't been for these kids, sir, the governor would be dead."

He paused and listened intently, and the look on his face made me start to hope again. "Yes, sir. Right, sir. That's great, sir—thank you!"

He hung up and turned to Sherlock. "Chief says I can make a copy of the tape first thing in the morning, before the agent picks it up. I'll show it to you on my VCR tomorrow night. But, Sherlock, you can't keep the tape. How's that? It's the best I can do."

Sherlock looked relieved. "Good enough," he answered. "Thanks, Officer Bill."

We said goodnight to Officer Bill, and Sherlock walked me back to my house. "We've got to do something, Sherlock," I pleaded. "They're gonna try to give Gimpy twenty years or more! And I don't believe he even did it!"

Sherlock shook his head. "He didn't."

I looked at him in surprise. "You sound pretty sure."

"I already have several clues. That wasn't Gimpy's car that we saw in the robbery. But I'm going to need a lot of evidence before the police are going to believe an eleven-year-old detective."

"How do you know it wasn't Gimpy's car?" I argued, as if I was suddenly on the side against Gimpy. "That was his license number."

Sherlock nodded. "I know," he replied, "but it wasn't Gimpy's car. Tomorrow, I'm hoping to get the proof we need. We need to bike out to Gimpy's place first thing in the morning, before they impound his car. Will you go with me?"

"Of course!" I agreed readily. "What time?"

"Six o'clock sharp," he said.

I stared at him in the darkness. "Six o'clock? Sherlock, you're crazy! I never get up that early, especially in the summer!"

He shrugged. "It's for Gimpy," he said. "There's a lot at stake here."

"All right," I said, stepping up on the porch. "But I hope you can prove he's innocent."

"We will," he answered simply. "Trust me. See you at six."

He turned and disappeared into the darkness, and I headed into the house.

I had a hard time getting to sleep that night.

FOUR

WE CHECK GIMPY'S CAR

I was asleep when a rock hit my bedroom window. With a *plink* it bounced off the glass. I sat there in bed, rubbing my eyes. A second rock bounced off the pane. This time I sprang out of bed, afraid that Sherlock would put the next one right through the glass.

Throwing up the sash, I leaned out my second-story window. Sherlock was down below on our front lawn, his right arm cocked for another throw. "Don't throw any more," I hissed. "The second one almost broke my window!"

"That wasn't the second one," he called up to me. "It was the fourteenth! You sure are hard to wake up!"

"I'll be down in a minute," I answered, and closed the window as quietly as I could, hoping we hadn't already wakened the whole house. I slithered out of the silly teddy bear nightgown that Aunt Emily had sent me last Christmas, hoping that Sherlock hadn't seen it. I dressed quickly, downed a glass of milk in the kitchen and then hurried out the back door to get my bike.

Sherlock already had it in the driveway. "You didn't have breakfast, did you?" he greeted me.

"Of course not," I answered sleepily. "I just woke up."

"Here." He pulled a small white bag from the basket on his handlebars and handed it to me. "Two sausage biscuits and an orange juice," he said. "It's a long ride out there to Gimpy's."

I took the bag and stared at him. This guy thinks of everything. "Thanks," I mumbled.

Steering with one hand, I ate my breakfast as we rode. I spilled half of the orange juice on my shirt, but everything tasted fantastic. When I had finished, I threw the bag of trash in the bushes at the edge of the road, but Sherlock made me go back and get it. "Responsible citizens never litter," he chided.

We pedaled slowly up Buffalo Ridge, huffing and puffing as we rode. Finally Sherlock stopped for a breather about two-thirds of the way up. "Let me ask you something," I panted. "How did you always know when Miss Wiggins was going to give a pop quiz?"

Sherlock just smiled. "You know some of my methods of investigation," he replied. "Figure it out."

"Sherlock," I was frustrated with him. "Come on! I have been trying to figure it out. I've been trying all year! But you always knew as soon as we walked into class if we were going to have a quiz."

Sherlock fiddled with the kickstand on his bike. "You saw exactly what I saw in class," he insisted. "Think!"

"But I can't do it like you can," I argued. "Come on, how did you know?"

He sighed, as though he was bored with the whole subject. "Miss Wiggins never prepared in advance, right?"

I nodded. "She was a regular procrastinator."

"And the quizzes were always written in long hand and duplicated on the school's old photocopier, right?"

I nodded, remembering the smudged writing that was always so hard to read, especially in Miss Wiggins's handwriting.

"Well, doesn't that tell you anything?"

"Not really," I answered. "Did you see her write the quizzes out?"

"No, Penny." He sighed again. "That old copier was always messy, and it always got toner all over everything. It's almost impossible to wash off. Each time we walked into class, I'd just look at Miss Wiggins's hands. If they had toner on them, she had been at the photocopier that day, and we were going to have a quiz. She never used that machine for anything else."

"Oh." I was disappointed. He always made it sound so easy, but when I try to use his methods of reasoning to figure things out, it comes out all wrong.

We reached Gimpy's place about half an hour later. He lives in a small white house, set back from the road, hidden from view by a thick grove of pines. A narrow lane with ruts nearly a foot deep led us on a meandering course back to his place.

"Good!" Sherlock called as we rode into the yard. "His car's still here! I was afraid that they would take it last night." I glanced over, and sure enough, the big green Impala was resting under the shade of an elm.

Sherlock hopped off his bike, popped the kickstand down, and then pulled a camera from the sack in his bike basket. "What's that for?" I asked.

"Evidence," he answered. "By the time the detectives get through with this car, a lot of the clues will be messed up. This thing has a close-up lens, so I hope it will get what I want."

The camera looked expensive. "What does a camera like that cost?" I asked.

"A little over five hundred dollars," he replied, squinting at the back of the Impala through the viewfinder. "I got it from Mr. Lewis. I traded him a network router that I found out at the dump and was able to fix."

I grinned. That was Sherlock for you!

Sherlock started snapping pictures of the rear of Gimpy's car. After several shots, he changed lenses, moved closer, and started shooting again. I watched him for a while, and then asked, "What are you taking pictures of?"

He glanced up briefly and then put his eye to the viewfinder again. "Evidence," he replied.

I shook my head. "I don't understand."

He shot two more exposures then set the camera in the basket on his bike and turned to face me. "Remember the picture that we looked at last night?"

I nodded.

"Maybe you noticed in the picture what I noticed at the time of the robbery."

I shook my head. I still had no idea what he was talking about.

"Penny," he said eagerly, "the back of the getaway car was spattered with mud. The entire bumper was covered with it, but the license plate was clean! It's really obvious in the picture Mrs. Abernathy took. What does that tell you?"

I shrugged. "They cleaned the license plate before the robbery?"

"No." I could tell he was trying to be patient with me, but was having a hard time of it. "The license plate was relatively clean because they had just taken it from another car. Gimpy's car."

I stared at him.

"Penny, the robbers took the license plate from Gimpy's car, put it on the back of their own car, which is the same year, model, and color as Gimpy's, and pulled off the bank robbery with Gimpy's license plate on their car!"

I frowned. "Why would they do that?"

"To throw the police off their trail. They committed the robbery in broad daylight. Someone was bound to get their license number; in fact, they were hoping for that. When the police trace the license number—bingo! They arrest Gimpy!"

"How would they get the plate from his car?"

"Penny, think. Where was Gimpy all day yesterday?"

"Fishing."

"Exactly! And where was he fishing? Where else, but his favorite hole, at the junction of Miner's Creek and Wahala River. Everyone in town knows about Gimpy's secret fishing spot. The robbers found his car in the willows in the creek bottom at the end of Mockingbird Lane, where he always parks it. They took his license plate, put it on the back of their own car, pulled the bank job, then returned to Gimpy's car to replace the plate."

"Why would they bother to do all that?" I asked. "After the bank job, why didn't they just toss Gimpy's license plate somewhere alongside the highway, and get out of town?"

"Because they wanted to put the bloodhounds on Gimpy's trail!"

"Bloodhounds?"

"The police investigators. If Gimpy's license plate was missing, the case against him wouldn't be as strong."

I thought it through, and it made sense. "How do we prove it?" I asked.

"That's why we're here now. I think I got all the proof I need."

I was still in the dark. "Show me what you're talking about," I begged.

He pointed to the back tires of Gimpy's Impala. "What do you see?"

"Tires."

"Yes, but what type of tires?"

How was I to know what he was talking about? "Uh, Goodyear," I said.

"Penny, they're snow tires! Gimpy never changes them!" His voice rose in pitch as he got excited. "The tires on the getaway car were not snow tires. They were regular radials!"

"Are you sure?"

"Of course, I'm sure!" he exploded. "I saw them at the robbery, and you can see them in Mrs. Abernathy's picture too. Gimpy's car was not the getaway car."

He pointed to the red plastic lens of the left taillight. "Did you notice the hole?"

I nodded, pleased that I had at least seen that. "It was in the picture last night," I said.

He shook his head. "No, that was the getaway car," he said. "The hole is in the same basic spot, but it's shaped slightly different. I think the bank robbers made the hole on purpose, probably with a screwdriver."

"Why would they do that?"

"Because Gimpy's taillight has a broken lens. Remember, they're trying to make people think that their car was Gimpy's."

I was amazed. First, at Sherlock's brilliant detective work, and second, at the great lengths the robbers had gone to. "These guys are sharp," I said.

He smiled grimly. "Yes, but not sharp enough."

He put the camera carefully back in its case and then walked back to where I was standing by the car. He pointed to the license plate. "Look at the license," he instructed. "It's got a light residue of dust and road film, but it's not caked with mud like the back of the getaway car."

I reached out to touch the plate, and he grabbed my arm. "Don't!" I jerked my hand back as though I had been burned.

"Sorry," he apologized, "I didn't mean to startle you. But it's very important that we not touch this plate." He looked at me. "You saw the picture of this plate when it was on the getaway car, right?"

I nodded.

"What's different about it now?"

"It's on a different car," I laughed.

"No, what's different about it?" he persisted.

I didn't know.

"Penny, this license plate is secured by two screws at the top." I looked, and of course, he was right.

"So?"

"The license plate in the photo had no screws showing. I think they secured it on with tape—probably duct tape—on the back of the plate."

He anticipated my next question and answered it before I could open my mouth. "Because it would be the fastest way to get it off after the robbery. But they took the time to put it back on Gimpy's car with screws, so it wouldn't be suspicious when the police investigated it. But they just put it on with two screws and tossed the other two away."

"How do you know that there were four screws before?" I asked.

He pointed to the two lower corners of the plate. "Don't touch it," he warned again, "but tell me what you see."

I squatted down behind the car and leaned close to the license plate. "There's a clean circle around the little hole in each corner," I observed.

"Right," he answered. "And there are some faint scratches around the outside of the circle. The clean places show that there were screws in these holes until recently. The scratches are from the tool that they used to take the screws out, a wrench or a socket. I'm going to suggest to Officer Bill that the police check the spot where Gimpy's car was parked yesterday. I'll bet anything they find both screws within thirty yards of there."

"Suppose they can't find where he parked?" I asked.

"It's easy to find," he retorted. "I was out there this morning."

I laughed. "You were at my house at six!"

He nodded. "But I went to Mockingbird Lane first. I started working as soon as it was light enough to shoot. I got pictures of the tracks in the road and everything. You can see where Gimpy parked, where the other Impala pulled in before the robbery to get the license plate, and when they came back to return it."

My eyes widened in surprise. "You can tell all that?"

He chuckled. "It was easy. That's a dirt road, and Gimpy's car had snow tires, while the getaway car didn't. Anyone could read what happened there!"

Anyone named Sherlock, I thought to myself.

FIVE

THE VIDEO

Sherlock came over after supper, and we headed over to Officer Bill's to see the video from the robbery. Sherlock was so excited he could hardly stand it. We knocked on Officer Bill's door, and the big police officer opened it immediately. "Come in," he greeted us, "I've been expecting you."

We followed him into the living room to find that he already had the TV on and the VCR tape cued to the proper starting point.

"The bank camera takes one still picture every ninety seconds automatically," Officer Bill explained. "But when activated, the camera functions like a regular video camera."

He gestured toward the couch. "Have a seat. I'll start the film. You'll see a couple of the stills that were taken; then the video kicks in when the teller saw the robbers and turned on the camera."

THE VIDEO

He started the film. For a few seconds, we saw a picture of the inside of the bank, facing the front door. One or two customers were in the bank. The picture blinked, and the image of a bearded man holding a shotgun appeared in the entrance. The camera shutter had clicked at the instant he walked in. The second robber was not yet in the bank. The picture blinked again, and suddenly, there was motion.

The two robbers were halfway across the bank when the video started to roll. As we expected, the film showed that both men were bearded and both carried weapons. The man with the revolver was limping. "It does look like Gimpy, except for the beard," I remarked, but the others were intent on watching the film.

The men walked off the lower edge of the screen as they moved out of camera angle. We saw a female customer run and hide behind a desk. Seconds later Mr. Phillips appeared on the screen, his revolver drawn and ready, intending to stop the robbers when they came out of the vault area.

Suddenly Mr. Phillips raised his gun slightly, and in the same instant, his body jerked upwards and backwards. I gave a little scream as I realized that he had just been shot. He fell to the floor, twisted sideways, and then lay still.

The two bearded robbers reappeared, this time heading toward the door. They both carried white canvas bank bags. Clutching the bank bag in his left hand, the man with the shotgun suddenly whirled around, his weapon thrust out in front of him. For about three seconds, he was facing directly toward the camera. He swung the shotgun from side to side, apparently making sure that no one was attempting to follow them, and then hurried to catch up with his partner, who was limping toward the front door. The door closed behind the men, but the camera continued to roll.

"Rewind it, and let's watch it again," Sherlock requested. Moments later, we were watching the same scenario all over again. I covered my eyes when it came to the part where Mr. Phillips was shot.

The phone rang, and Officer Bill handed the VCR remote to Sherlock. "Here," he said. "Rewind it again if you want. I've got to catch the phone." He hurried into the kitchen.

Sherlock rewound the film and watched it again, pausing it occasionally to study a particular image, sometimes playing it in slow motion. Officer Bill came back into the room several minutes later.

"Well, pal, did you learn anything?" he asked with a grin. "We've watched that tape a dozen times at the station, but we've still not learned much from it."

Sherlock smiled at that. "This tape is loaded with clues," he stated. "I think I've learned enough from it to catch these guys."

Officer Bill laughed out loud. "Come on, Sherlock," he snickered, "don't tell me you're seeing things in this tape that we overlooked. We're the professionals, and you're just a kid!"

I glanced at Sherlock, but he didn't seem at all upset by Officer Bill's put-down. He picked up the remote control again and rewound the tape, with the images flitting backwards across the screen.

"Both the beards are fake," he said.

Officer Bill nodded. "We figured that, but there's no way to prove it."

"The tape proves it," Sherlock claimed.

"Nah," Officer Bill replied impatiently. "There's no way to prove that from the tape."

"Sure, there is," the boy detective insisted. He started the tape playing on slow speed, and we saw the bank robbers walking toward the camera. When the man in front was looking toward the camera, Sherlock froze the picture on the screen.

"The picture is really clear," I commented, "for a freeze frame."

"It's an expensive VCR," Sherlock told me.

He studied the man's face on the screen for a moment and then turned to me. "Officer Bill hasn't shaved since this morning," he said. "I think he's got enough stubble for me to show you something. Penny, look at Officer Bill's chin. Now, does his beard actually touch his lower lip?"

I reached out one finger and touched Officer Bill's chin, just below his lower lip. "No," I answered, "there's about an eighth of an inch between his lip and the place where his beard starts."

Sherlock nodded. "Right," he agreed, as if he had just examined Officer Bill's face with me. "Officer Bill, if you want to see what we're talking about, take a look in the mirror. You'll see that your beard does not touch your lip."

"I've noticed that before," the policeman said, "but what does that prove?"

Sherlock pointed to the face on the screen. "Look at his beard. It's up a little too high, and actually covers the edge of his lower lip. There's not a man in the world that grows whiskers right on his lips. This beard is fake!"

"Let me show you something else," he continued. He advanced the tape for a few more seconds and then paused it when the other robber's face was visible. "Study this man's face," he suggested. "Notice especially how his beard is positioned."

We studied the picture for about thirty seconds, and then Sherlock advanced the tape again. He slowed it down as the men emerged from the vault area, then put it on pause when the man with the revolver glanced in the direction of the camera for just a second.

"Look at his face, now," he said. "Remember how the beard looked before? See the difference?"

Officer Bill and I studied the screen for several moments, and then suddenly I saw what Sherlock was trying to point out. "You can see more of his mouth," I said. "The beard looks like it's slightly lower now."

Officer Bill nodded. "You're right!"

"See what I mean?" Sherlock said triumphantly. "The beards are fake. The tape proves it. I figure they probably itch and are uncomfortable. When the robber was in the vault area, out of sight of the camera, he either scratched it with his hand or rubbed it on his shoulder. When he did, he moved it slightly out of position. Not much, but just enough to notice if you were looking for it."

Officer Bill laughed. "Sorry, Sherlock, I was wrong. You've proved that they had fake beards. What else can you tell from the tape?"

"Well," Sherlock answered, "the man with the limp is not Gimpy. The limp is faked."

"Yeah," I said, "he didn't limp when he ran out of the bank!"

Officer Bill shook his head. "Maybe you just didn't notice it at the time," he argued. "The limp looks real to me."

"It's not," Sherlock declared. "Want me to prove it?"

Officer Bill just waved his hand. "Go ahead."

Sherlock rewound the tape to the point where the robbers had just come in the door. The second man in, the one with the revolver, limped across the bank.

"It looks real to me," I decided.

"He's practiced it a few times," Sherlock replied. "But he messed up. Watch this."

He fast-forwarded the tape to the part where the robbers were heading toward the door, away from the vault. We watched in silence as the robbers left the bank. As before, the man with the revolver was limping.

"Did you catch it?" Sherlock asked, looking from Officer Bill to me.

We both shook our heads.

"He limps on his right leg, like Gimpy does," Sherlock said. "It's a pretty convincing limp. He's practiced it quite a bit. But when he came back out from the vault, he limped on his left!"

He played both parts of the tape again, and sure enough, he was right.

Officer Bill slapped his leg in disgust. "If that doesn't beat all!" he said. "We watched that tape at the station a dozen times, and not one of us noticed that!"

Sherlock looked at him. "Still believe that's Gimpy?" He pulled out the snapshots of Gimpy's Impala—he had had them developed at a one-hour photo place—and began to explain about the license plate switch.

As Officer Bill studied the photographs, Sherlock explained his theory, pointing out the various bits of evidence in the snapshots. When he had finished, Officer Bill looked at Sherlock with a new respect in his eyes.

"You're a genius, Sherlock!" he exclaimed in amazement. "Mind if I keep these? I'll show them to Chief in the morning."

Sherlock nodded. "No problem," he said. "Just make sure they come back to me when you're through with them, OK?"

We left a few minutes later. As we walked back to my house, Sherlock was deep in thought, and I knew his mind was working on something else he had seen in the bank robbery video, probably something that Officer Bill and I had not even noticed.

"Whatcha thinking about?" I asked, but I don't think he even heard my question.

"Penny, we've got some work to do tomorrow," he said absently. "I'll see you first thing in the morning."

With that he was gone.

SIX

WE INVESTIGATE

The next morning, there was a knock at the front door. Dad was just leaving for work, so he answered the door on his way out. I had my mouth full of English muffin (they're really fantastic with cream cheese) when Sherlock appeared in the kitchen.

"Good morning, Sherlock," Mom greeted him. "Care for a glass of orange juice?"

Sherlock shook his head. "No, thank you, Mrs. Gordon."

Mom didn't give up. "Scrambled eggs then? Sausage? English muffin?"

Sherlock shook his head at each of Mom's offerings. "No, thank you," he said politely. "We already had breakfast."

Mom tossed her curly red head and said impishly, "That's the first time I've ever seen this boy when he wasn't hungry!"

It was true. Sherlock was never one to turn down anything to eat. I knew that he was impatient to get working on some new clue regarding the case of the bank robbery.

He sat down across the table from me, and I could tell that he was immensely pleased about something. "Good news," he said. "They released Gimpy a while ago. Officer Bill and Chief Ramsey went out to Mockingbird Lane with a metal detector early this morning. They found the two missing screws from Gimpy's license plate, and the chief agreed that my theory was right after he had studied the tire tracks out there."

"All on account of your detective work, I assume," Mom commented. "Penny's been telling us all about it." Mom's a big fan of Sherlock's.

"She helped too," Sherlock said, generously.

"I didn't do anything," I protested. "I've just been along to watch." But inside, I was pleased that Sherlock had included me in the credit.

I turned to him. "You've done it," I said excitedly. "You solved the bank robbery case in just two days!"

He shook his head. "All we've done is prove Gimpy innocent," he replied. "We still have a lot to do. We have to identify the robbers and assist the police in apprehending them. And we still have to recover the missing $180,000."

"I'm afraid I can't go with you this morning," I said, doing a poor job of hiding my disappointment. "I've been letting my chores pile up the last couple of days, and Mom's gonna skin me alive if I don't get on them."

My pretty mother waved her hand at me. "Oh, go ahead, Penny," she urged. "See this thing through to the end. I can always skin you later." Her brown eyes twinkled.

That was all I needed to hear. "Thanks, Mom!" I nearly shouted. I hugged her, and moments later Sherlock and I were pedaling into town.

"Where are we going?" I called to Sherlock, whose bike was a hundred feet ahead of mine. He slowed slightly so that my bike could pull alongside.

"I want to interview Mr. Gillis," he answered, "and get some more details on the robbery. Then I figure we need to ride out to the welders' union. It's in Spencerville, about ten or twelve miles from here."

I was puzzled. "Why are we going to the welders' union?" I asked. "What has that got to do with the robbery?"

But he just shook his head. "You'll see," he said.

The bank had just opened when we got there. We parked our bikes on the sidewalk just to the left of the door, in the very spot where we had stood as the robbers made their getaway. I stood for a moment recalling the events of the robbery, and a thrill of horror swept over me. Somehow it now seemed so long ago.

I followed Sherlock into the bank, and he approached the receptionist. "We need to see Mr. Gillis, please," he said politely, handing her a business card. We could see Mr. Gillis through the open door of his office.

As we watched, the receptionist entered Mr. Gillis's office, said something to him, and handed him Sherlock's card. He looked up, saw us, and shook his head. We could see his lips move as he handed the card back to her, but we couldn't hear what he said.

The lady was very apologetic when she came back out. "I'm sorry, but Mr. Gillis is very busy right now," she said. "The police investigators are coming again this morning, and he doesn't have time for a couple of kids."

I turned to go, but Sherlock stood his ground. He pulled something from his pocket, and I saw that it was his savings account passbook.

"Miss Gordon and I are bank customers," he said in a businesslike tone. "We both have accounts here. Our families have accounts here. Our accounts will remain here, as long as we can see Mr. Gillis. We only need three minutes of his time."

She entered the office again, and we could see that Mr. Gillis was irritated as she talked to him, but he finally agreed to see us. He greeted us coldly as we entered.

"Good morning, Mr. Gillis," Sherlock said cheerfully, as if we had just received a warm reception. "We need about three minutes of your time; then we'll get out of your hair."

He asked to see the vault area, where the robbers had actually gotten their hands on the money. Our reluctant host started to refuse, then shrugged, and led us to the back of the bank. I think he had decided that he could get rid of Sherlock most easily by complying with his wishes. Whatever the reason, he did take us back there. He showed us a small office, located right beside the main vault.

"This is where the money is counted and receipted after an armored delivery," he told us. "On the day in question, I had just confirmed and recorded the delivery. A large amount of cash was involved, as we were handling the Reynolds' plant payroll. The Keepsafe truck had been gone about ten minutes. I had just opened the vault when the two men burst into the room, forced me against the wall at gunpoint, and took the cash from the desk. When I turned around, they were gone."

"Was the money delivered in white canvas bags?" Sherlock asked.

The man shook his head. "It was in large, flat, covered plastic trays," he replied.

"Where did the robbers get the bags then?"

"They were in the bottom of this cabinet," the manager answered. "They opened the cabinet, grabbed the sacks, and loaded the deposit into them."

"How did they know the bags were there?" Sherlock asked.

The man shrugged. "We don't know. Customers are seldom allowed back here."

"Does the vault have a timer?" Sherlock asked.

The manager nodded. "You're a smart young man," he commented. "There is a twenty-minute release period each morning, and another one in the afternoon. No one can open the vault at any other time—myself included. The Keepsafe deliveries have to be made during one of those two times."

"Are the release periods ever varied from time to time?" the young detective asked.

Mr. Gillis shook his head. "They were set a little over two years ago, when we installed the new vault," he answered. "We didn't see any need to rotate the schedule, but of course that's changed now."

"Then the robbers must have been familiar with the schedule," Sherlock observed.

"They were familiar with everything!" the man exploded. "They were familiar with the layout of the bank, the timing of the delivery, where the bags were kept, everything! We figure it has to be an inside job."

"Are there any employees, or past employees, that you would suspect?"

Mr. Gillis shook his head emphatically. "None," he stated. "In the past fifteen years, this bank has only had eleven different employees, including me. Eight of them work here now, and two of the other three are dead. There's not a chance that either of the robbers has ever worked here, but it sure looks that way. They knew what they were doing."

Sherlock held out a skinny hand. "Thanks for your help, Mr. Gillis."

Sherlock was quiet as we walked out to our bikes.

"Well, you tried," I told him, "even if we didn't learn anything."

He looked at me in surprise. "We learned plenty!" he declared. "Mr. Gillis was more helpful than I had expected."

"I think he just wanted to get rid of us," I said with a laugh, "and he figured that the fastest way was to humor you."

Sherlock shrugged. "At least he took the time to talk with us."

We pedaled west out of town, past my house, then past his. Sherlock hadn't said a word since we left the bank, and I knew better than to interrupt his thinking. I knew that somehow he had picked up some new clues from our interview with Mr. Gillis, but I had no idea what they were.

Finally we pulled off to the side of the road for a rest, and he seemed ready to reveal his plans. "After we visit the welders' union, we need to go out to the Keepsafe headquarters," he said.

"Where's that?" I asked.

"East of Willoughby, about ten miles," he answered.

"But that's miles in the other direction," I protested.

He nodded. "I hope you had a good breakfast. It's going to be a long day."

We didn't get very far at the welders' union. Sherlock told the receptionist that we needed to see a union rep, (short for representative, I think), and she led us into a smoke-filled office. A mean-looking man sat behind a huge desk, puffing on a cigar. He stood up as we entered the untidy office.

Sherlock got right to the point. "We'd like to see the rolls of all your union members, please," he said.

The man blinked in surprise, but turned obediently to a file cabinet, flipped through it, and pulled out a folder. He opened the folder, laid it on his desk, then removed the cigar from his mouth, and spoke for the first time. "Here it is," he said gruffly.

The file in question looked like it had about fifteen or twenty pages in it. I could see that the top page was a computer printout, listing names, addresses, and phone numbers. I'd estimate that there were about twelve or fourteen names to the page.

"Thank you, sir," Sherlock said, as he reached for the documents.

"Wait a minute. What am I doing?" the union rep exclaimed. He snatched the folder from my friend's hands. "Who are you, anyway?" he growled.

Sherlock neatly sidestepped the question. "We need these records for a project that we're working on," he explained vaguely.

"Get lost, kid," the man growled again. He turned, opened the file drawer, and thrust the folder back into it. He turned back, pointed the cigar at me, and said, "You, too, missy. Beat it. You two don't have any business in these offices. So don't come back." He followed us to the outside door.

We pedaled meekly back to Sherlock's house. Sherlock didn't say a word during the whole trip. I felt kind of sorry for him.

Mrs. Jones fixed us some lunch, but while I was eating, Sherlock grabbed a long telephone cord and headed out the back door. I knew he had gone to his office.

Fifteen minutes later, he sauntered back in the kitchen with a pleased expression on his face. I had no idea who he had called, but apparently he had learned something.

We finished lunch and then rode east to the Keepsafe armored truck offices. Sherlock had a flat package in his bike basket. I was dying with curiosity, but I knew that he would not show it to me until he was ready. We finally reached our destination and parked our bikes at the edge of a gravel parking lot. Sherlock tucked the package under his arm, and we headed for the door.

As we reached the sidewalk, Sherlock stopped, opened the bag, and pulled out the object of my curiosity. It was a butterfly. Not just any butterfly, but the biggest butterfly I have ever seen. The thing was humongous, with a wingspan of nearly a foot! The creature was mounted in a walnut frame with a glass cover. It was resting against a backdrop of black velvet, which made the beautiful colors in the huge, magnificent wings jump right at you.

"This is a rare New Guinea Ornithoptera Alexandrae, or Queen Alexandra's Birdwing," he informed me. "It's the world's largest butterfly. This is a very unusual and valuable specimen. I was offered a hundred dollars for it once."

"What are you doing with it here?" I asked.

"I just learned that Tim Bradford's mother is the receptionist here at Keepsafe," he replied. "Tim has a small butterfly collection. He'd give his right arm to have this specimen."

"What are you going to do with it?" I asked.

"I'm going to give it to his mother to give to him," he answered. He didn't volunteer any more information, and I didn't push him.

I followed Sherlock into the Keepsafe building, and we found ourselves in a pleasant walnut-paneled reception area. There were a lot of windows, and the room was sunny and cheery. A large tropical fish tank was against one wall, and Sherlock stopped and peered into it for a moment, so I joined him.

"May I help you?" a pleasant voice asked, and we both turned to see a heavyset motherly-type lady standing before us. She looked friendly and cheerful. I had no idea what we were doing there, but I was hoping that Sherlock would fare better here than with the union rep.

"Mrs. Bradford?" Sherlock held out his hand politely. "I'm Jasper Jones. Most people call me Sherlock. Penelope and I go to school with your son, Tim."

Mrs. Bradford smiled. "Tim talks about you," she told the young detective. "Aren't you the one with the butterfly collection?"

As the woman glanced in my direction, Sherlock grinned and gave me the thumbs up sign.

"I'm the one with the butterflies," he admitted. "I brought something that I knew Tim would like." He pulled the magnificent butterfly from the bag, and Mrs. Bradford gasped when she saw it. "We didn't know where you live, so I thought I'd bring it out here, and ask you to give it to him."

The woman took the beautiful creature wordlessly, enamored by its beauty.

"Tim probably knows this," Sherlock told her, "but it's a New Guinea Ornithoptera Alexandrae, or Queen Alexandra's Birdwing. It's very rare and quite valuable. I'd like him to have it, but please, urge him to take care of it."

"Thank you, Sherlock," the woman breathed. She seemed awed by the gift of the huge butterfly.

"How long have you worked here?" Sherlock asked casually.

Mrs. Bradford's attention was still on the butterfly. "I've been here seven years," she answered.

"Do you have an exhaustive list of all the Keepsafe employees?" he asked.

"I'd have that on the computer," she answered.

"Would it have employees from two or three years ago?"

"I haven't purged the files since I've worked here," the friendly woman answered, "so they would show every employee of Keepsafe for at least the last seven years."

I held my breath as Sherlock asked, "Are you allowed to give out that information?"

She shrugged. "I don't see why not. It's not classified, you know."

"Would it be too much trouble to get a printout of that?" Sherlock queried.

"No, no trouble at all," she answered, and Sherlock flashed me a victory smile. I still didn't know what he was after, but I sensed that the roster he wanted was somehow very important to our investigation.

Mrs. Bradford didn't even ask him what he wanted the printout for, but she simply walked over to her desk and punched a command or two into the computer keyboard. The printer came to life and began to hum as it recorded the information that Sherlock had requested. Mrs. Bradford picked up the huge butterfly and admired it all over again while we waited.

Minutes later, she handed a computer printout of moderate length to Sherlock and thanked him repeatedly for coming. We thanked her for her help and headed for our bikes, Sherlock clutching the precious Keepsafe employee records.

"You got it!" I exulted, as we pedaled toward home.

He laughed happily. "Butterflies are attracted to flowers," he chuckled, "and sometimes people are attracted to butterflies!"

"But you gave up your best specimen," I lamented.

He shrugged. "Someday I'll get another one," he said simply. "If this investigation pans out, it'll be worth it."

"Why is the Keepsafe employee record so valuable to you?" I asked. "I'm not following you at all on this case!"

He frowned, pedaling along for a moment or two in silence. Then he answered, "It's not worth anything to me unless we get the welders' union records to go with it. Penny, we have to go out there again tomorrow!"

I shrank back from the idea. "We'll just get thrown out again," I warned. "Why even try?"

We had reached Willoughby by then, and I looked up to realize that we were pedaling past the bank at that moment. Moments later, we turned into the dirt lane leading to my house. Sherlock braked to a stop, so I did likewise.

"Come over to my house tomorrow at nine," he said. "I'll meet you in my office. We'll bike out to the union hall again. Things will be different tomorrow, I promise." He waved and rode down the highway.

I pedaled down our lane, my bike tires occasionally shooting pieces of gravel. Sure, it will be different tomorrow! I thought to myself. If we go back in that union rep's office, we'll probably both be dead!

I decided to try to talk Sherlock out of going back.

SEVEN

PRAYER MEETING

That evening after supper, Mom, Dad, and I headed for the Wednesday night prayer service at our church. As Dad slowed the car to turn into the church parking lot, he remarked, "You know what I heard at work today? Gimpy Williams was released this morning! Lack of evidence, or something."

I spoke up. "It wasn't a lack of evidence, Dad. It was new evidence that showed that Gimpy was not involved in the robbery. He's innocent."

Dad frowned. "I thought they had pretty solid proof that he was involved, Penny. I understand that there was a photo of the getaway car showing his license number. That would be pretty solid evidence, I'd say." He maneuvered the car into a parking space.

"The license plate in the photo was Gimpy's," I replied, "but the car wasn't."

Dad shut off the engine and turned to look at me. "Say that again? I didn't follow you."

"The robbers switched license plates with Gimpy before the bank robbery," I explained, "and then put Gimpy's plate back on his car after the robbery just to make the police think that Gimpy had done it."

Dad was still frowning. "Where did you hear that, Penny? That story seems a bit far-fetched."

"It's true," I insisted. "Sherlock proved it to the police, and that's why they released Gimpy!" I told the whole story about going out to Gimpy's place to get pictures of his car, the broken taillights, and everything.

When I finished, Dad let out a low whistle. "That's incredible," he said quietly. "Your friend Sherlock never misses a single detail, does he?"

"Not usually," I answered proudly.

"This is really going to shake some people up," Dad said. "Most folks in town are convinced that Gimpy is guilty. The office staff talked of nothing else today. Most people were pretty upset that Gimpy was released."

"The shoppers in Smedley's Grocery were all talking about it today too," Mom reported. "Everyone's pretty well convinced that Gimpy was one of the gunmen who robbed the bank. It's as if he's already been convicted without a trial."

"He didn't do it, Mom!" I exclaimed. "Sherlock has the proof that Gimpy didn't do it! And that's why the police released him this morning!"

"I believe you, Penny," Mom replied quietly, as she looked in the mirror on her sun visor and smoothed down her curls. She opened her door. "Well, let's go to church."

Mom and Dad headed for the main auditorium, where the adults meet for prayer meeting, and I hurried on toward the educational building, where the young people my age have class. I stepped up on the sidewalk, hurried around the corner of the building, and almost ran smack into a man standing by the shrubbery. To my surprise, it was Gimpy.

"Gimpy!" I exclaimed. "Sherlock told me that you had been released. I'm glad that the police realized that you didn't do it!"

He looked at me with a mixture of surprise and pain reflected in his sad eyes. "Are you sure I didn't do it, Penny Loafer?" he said quietly. "Everyone else in town seems to think that I did."

"Sherlock proved that you didn't do it," I told him resolutely. "That's good enough for me. And besides, I already knew that you would never rob a bank. I knew that before Sherlock ever showed me how the real robbers had switched license plates."

Gimpy dropped his head. "Thank you, Penny. I just wish other folks had that much confidence in me."

"What are you doing out here?" I questioned. "The service is about to start, you know."

He sighed. "I'm just trying to decide whether or not I'm going in," he replied quietly.

I looked at him in alarm. "Decide if you're going in?" I echoed. "Why wouldn't you go in?"

"Some folks don't seem to want me around right now."

"Gimpy," I scolded, "this is your church. Of course, they want you!"

He shook his head. "Some people don't. They seem to want to believe the rumors that are going around town."

"Well, I believe in you, Gimpy," I told him stoutly. "And I think you'll find that most people in this church do too. They're your brothers and sisters in Christ. We're all family."

I was hardly prepared for what happened next. Mr. and Mrs. Portlock, an elderly couple in our church, happened along just then. Mr. Portlock always drives expensive cars and his wife always wears exotic clothes and flashy jewelry, so I suppose that they have a lot of money. I sometimes feel that they look down on most of us in the church because we're not as well off as they are. Anyway, when they passed us on the sidewalk, Mrs. Portlock stopped and stared at Gimpy as if she just couldn't believe what she was seeing.

"Mr. Williams," she said in a disapproving voice, "what do you think you're doing here? Aren't you supposed to be in jail?"

"Martha, be still," her husband whispered fiercely. "Come along now."

"No, Amos, I won't be still," the woman replied curtly. "Someone has to say it, and it might as well be me. We all know what this man did, and I for one am not going to just stand quietly by and let him get away with it."

I was boiling. "Mrs. Portlock," I fumed, so angry that I was trembling and yet trying to remember to be respectful at the same time, "Gimpy Williams had nothing to do with the bank robbery. He was framed! The police now have ample proof that he was not involved in any way."

Mrs. Portlock took half a step backwards and seemed to see me for the first time. "Young lady—Bertha, isn't it?—this man was seen driving the getaway car! He's as guilty as the devil!"

"Come along, Martha." Mr. Portlock made another feeble attempt to drag his wife away, but she was having none of it.

"Mrs. Portlock,"—I was so angry that I was crying now—"my name is Penny. My friend Sherlock Jones found proof that the getaway car did **not** belong to Gimpy! Gimpy is innocent. You've been listening to idle gossip, and you're ready to condemn an innocent man!"

"Well, I never!" Mrs. Portlock was clearly offended by my outburst. She took a small step toward me, opened her mouth as if to say something, and then just stood there. She glanced at her husband, then at me, and finally at Gimpy, all without saying a word.

After a few seconds of silence, she tried again. "Young lady, would your parents approve of you hobnobbing with the likes of this man? I think not!"

She pounced on Gimpy like a hawk on a field mouse. "Mr. Williams, we all know what you did. As a charter member of this church, I demand that you leave our young people alone! If I had the authority, I would order you off this property immediately!"

She turned to her husband. "Come along, Amos. We'll be late for the service."

As the Portlocks hurried toward the church auditorium, Gimpy looked at me with a pained expression. He turned both hands palms up in a helpless gesture of resignation. "See what I mean, Miss Penny? It's been like this all day. And I just can't go where I'm not wanted."

I grabbed his sleeve, but he pulled away. "Good night, Penny." Head down, he shuffled down the sidewalk, looking so forlorn that I actually hurt inside for him.

I hesitated just a moment and then ran after him. "Gimpy, wait!"

"Don't worry about me, Miss Penny," he said in a subdued voice, without turning. "I'll be all right. If these people don't want me, I don't need them."

I was struggling to hold back the tears as I hurried in front of Gimpy and blocked his path. "Wait, Gimpy," I pleaded. "Listen!"

He tried to sidestep me, but I grabbed him by both arms. "Gimpy, please! These people are your brothers and sisters in the Lord. You're part of a family. You can't just walk away!"

"If they don't want me here, Miss Penny, then I ain't about to stay."

"Most of them do want you, Gimpy. The only ones who don't want you here are the ones who were foolish enough to listen to idle gossip."

"Mrs. Portlock made it pretty clear that I'm not wanted."

"Then she's one of the foolish ones!" There—it was out. Maybe I shouldn't have said it that way, but that was exactly how I felt. "With an attitude like she just displayed, you and I both know that she can't be right with the Lord."

"I can't walk in there and have them all staring at me," Gimpy said quietly. "I . . . I just can't take that."

"Then I'm going with you!" I declared. "You can sit with my parents and me."

"Don't you have a class tonight?"

"I'll stay with the adults," I told him, "so that you don't have to walk in alone. Come on, church is just about to start."

To my surprise, he turned and accompanied me down the sidewalk. The service was just starting as we entered the sanctuary. Gimpy and I hurried down a side aisle and paused at the row where my parents were sitting.

"Excuse us, please," I whispered, squeezing past Mr. and Mrs. Anderson, a middle-aged couple who had taught Sunday school in our church for years and years. I slid into a seat beside Mom, and Gimpy settled in right beside me. Mom looked over and gave us both a warm smile.

"Welcome to our Wednesday evening prayer service," our music director said from the pulpit. "Let's take our hymn books and stand to sing hymn number eighty-nine."

As we stood to our feet, I sensed movement at the end of our pew and glanced in that direction. To my amazement, Mr. and Mrs. Anderson left our row and moved to a pew two rows behind us! I was shocked. I glanced at Gimpy and saw his lips tighten.

When we finished the first hymn, one of the deacons came to the pulpit and led in prayer. At the conclusion of the prayer, I glanced over at Gimpy, but he was no longer there. His spot was empty.

EIGHT

THE UNION HALL AGAIN

I pedaled into Sherlock's driveway at two minutes to nine. I had agreed to meet him in his office, so I headed around the side of the house, back to the little shed that served as headquarters to one of the most effective detective agencies ever in existence. Parking my bike in the shade of a towering magnolia, I went inside to meet Sherlock.

The little office was empty, so I sat down on one of the milk crate "chairs" to wait. I tried to figure out why the welders' union was so important to the robbery but saw no connection whatsoever. I was completely in the dark.

The door opened, and I jumped up. But it wasn't Sherlock. A skinny girl with pink-rimmed glasses walked in. She looked around her in disgust. She had the curliest hair I have ever seen and at least as many freckles as I do—probably more. She was wearing a pink wristwatch with little fake diamonds around the edge, and she glanced at it repeatedly. I figured she was about eight or nine years old.

Finally she seemed to notice my presence, and she walked over and stood before me. "I'm looking for Sherlock Jones," she announced in a tiny little voice. "Have you seen him?"

For some unknown reason, I felt irritated at this tiny little imp of a girl. She had merely asked a question, yet she seemed so arrogant, so demanding.

"I haven't seen him since yesterday," I replied. "I was supposed to meet him here at nine, so he should be here soon." I'm afraid I was a little impatient with her.

She sat down on a milk crate—my milk crate—and studied me with big owlish eyes. "Don't I know you from somewhere?" she asked in that tiny little mouse-like voice.

"I don't think so," I told her coldly. "I probably just look like someone else you know."

"Have you ever been to Abilene?" she asked.

"No," I answered, "I don't even know where that is!"

"I'm sure I've seen you before somewhere," she continued.

I turned back to her. "I don't think so," I replied, "because I've never seen you before!"

She fell silent, and I studied her while we waited. If Sherlock were here, he could find out all sorts of things about this child without even asking her a single question. I decided to pass the time by seeing what I could discover about her, just by observing her.

She appeared to come from a family that was fairly well off. Her clothes had designer labels, and she had fake, but obviously expensive, fingernails. I decided that she was probably from Florida or some other warm climate, as she shivered and seemed to be cold, even though it was June weather. Beyond that, I could tell very little about her.

"Are you Sherlock's girlfriend?" the little girl asked suddenly. The question took me by surprise.

"No!" I exclaimed. "We're just friends. Good friends. I'm too young to have a boyfriend."

We sat in silence for several more minutes. Suddenly I heard Sherlock's voice. "Well, we had better head for the welders' union, Penny."

I jumped to my feet then stopped, puzzled. The words had come from the lips of the thin little freckle-faced girl! While I watched in stunned amazement, she reached up and snatched off her curly hair, revealing the short hair of a boy. It was Sherlock!

I gaped at him, totally in shock. He grinned. "What do you think? Will anyone recognize me?"

I finally recovered enough to find my voice. "Put the wig back on, and your own mother won't recognize you!" I retorted. I was a little put out by his trick. It was embarrassing to think that he had fooled me so completely. But to be honest with you, the disguise was incredible, the best I had ever seen. And if he could fool me with it, he could fool anyone.

"How did you do the freckles?" I asked.

"Mom's eyeliner pencils," he grinned, trying to adjust the wig. "Do they look realistic?"

"Better than mine," I replied.

He turned toward the door of the little shed. "Let's head for the welder's union again."

I stared at him, aghast. "You're going out in public?" I shrilled. "Like that?"

He shrugged. "Why shouldn't I?" he answered. "I'm in disguise."

"I just thought you'd be embarrassed to be seen like that."

"Why should I?" he reasoned. "No one will know it's me."

I thought it through, and as usual, what he said made sense. When he rode out of the garage a moment later, I saw just how complete his disguise really was. He was riding a girl's bike!

I rode alongside Sherlock. "Gimpy was at church last night," I remarked.

"Good!" Sherlock exclaimed. "I was hoping he would come, but I was afraid that he might not. This whole town has been talking about the robbery, and most people are still convinced that Gimpy was one of the gunmen. The gossip has been fast and furious, and that can be hard to take if you're the object of it."

"He didn't stay," I said. "Oh, Sherlock, I was so embarrassed for him, and so hurt for him! People can be so cruel—even Christian people."

He rode closer to me. "What happened?"

"Mrs. Portlock told him that he was not welcome," I replied. "I had to talk him into coming into the service with me—I went to the adult service so that I could sit with him—and the Andersons deliberately moved to another pew so they wouldn't have to sit by him. Oh, Sherlock, it was awful! Gimpy left during the opening prayer."

Sherlock grimaced. "Idle tongues have been wagging all over town since the robbery. I guess I had hoped it would be different with believers, but it looks like I was wrong."

"But they're not even giving him a chance, Sherlock! The entire town of Willoughby has decided that he's guilty, and they're not even giving him a chance! You should have seen the hurt look on his face when Mrs. Portlock was chewing him out. I tried to stand up for him, but I don't think it did much good."

"You did what you could," my friend replied. "Thanks for trying. I wondered why you weren't in class last night."

"I hurt inside for Gimpy, and I'm so angry at these gossips that I could just—oh, I don't know what I could do!"

"They're using their tongues for evil, Penny, tearing others down instead of edifying and building others up. I'm disappointed that the believers in this town are behaving just as badly as the unsaved."

We rode in silence for awhile and finally coasted to a stop in the parking lot of the union offices. "I'll go in alone," Sherlock informed me. "You wait out here. If anyone sees us together, it will blow my cover. Pray that I get the info this time."

He parked his bike on the sidewalk and sauntered toward the front door, using the big glass windows as a mirror to adjust his skirt as he walked by. I began to ride in big circles around the parking lot. My heart was in my throat. What if they recognized Sherlock? What would they do to him?

Finally, after about a million circles around the parking lot, I parked my bike under the shade of a giant oak and lay on my back in the grass to wait for my partner. I glanced at my watch for the hundredth time. He had been gone for over fifteen minutes. Something must be wrong; he should have been out long before now.

I was trying to decide if I should dare to go inside and find Sherlock, or if I should ride to a phone and call the police for help, when the door opened, and out walked Sherlock. I was relieved to see that he was still alive, but to my dismay, I saw that his hands were empty. We had made the whole trip for nothing.

He climbed on his bike and rode from the parking lot without looking in my direction. I scrambled to my feet, hopped on my bike, and pedaled furiously to catch up. Finally, nearly half a mile down the highway, I caught him.

"Wait up, Sherlock," I puffed, as soon as I was within earshot of him. "Let me catch up!"

He slowed slightly, and I rode alongside. "Couldn't get the membership rolls, huh?" I sympathized. "Too bad."

He gave me a reproachful look. "Of course I got them," he replied. "That's what we came out here for, wasn't it?"

"Then, where are they?" I queried. "That folder was too big to stick in your pocket."

"I'm having them sent on ahead," he said. Seeing the puzzled look on my face, he called, "I'll explain when we stop at the top of the ridge for a break."

We pedaled to the top of the next hill, and Sherlock pulled off to the side of the road for a breather. I waited expectantly for his account of what had transpired in the union office.

"I had the membership rolls sent to Officer Bill's office," he told me triumphantly. "We'll pick them up when we get into town. I can't wait to get my hands on them!"

"What do you mean?" I asked. "How did you get them to agree to send the information to the police station?"

Sherlock chuckled as he wiped off his freckles. "They don't know that's where they're sending it," he said. Then he told the story of what had taken place while I was waiting outside.

"Remember the row of big green chairs across from the receptionist's desk?" he asked. "Well, I sat down in one of those, and the receptionist asked if she could help me. She was really busy taking phone calls and stuff, so I replied that I was just waiting.

"I sat there for about twenty minutes, and finally things slowed down a bit for her. As soon as I saw that she had a bit of a break, I approached the receptionist and asked her if she would have the union records on computer. She said that she did, and I told her that I needed them for a project I was working on. I gave her the fax number at the police station, and she agreed to fax them there. She didn't ask what I needed them for."

I marveled at Sherlock's boldness. "Why would she even agree to do that?" I mused. "Most adults would never do something like that for a kid."

He lifted one hand and fluffed his wig. "I'm a cute kid," he replied, in his little girl voice.

"Oh, brother," I groaned.

He grinned. "It worked, didn't it?"

"I'm just glad that you didn't get yourself shot!"

He climbed on his bike. "We'd better hurry to the police station," he said. "The fax will be there now, and Chief Ramsey will have no idea what it's for." He smiled in anticipation. "In just a few minutes, I'll be able to name one of the bank robbers!"

We coasted down the hill. I was as confused as ever. Sherlock was acting as though the case was practically solved, and I still had no idea what was going on! I pedaled hard to catch up again.

NINE

A SECOND ARREST

When we entered the police station, the entire Willoughby police force—all three of them—was clustered around the fax machine in Officer Bill's office. Chief Ramsey had a sheaf of papers in his hands, and I knew immediately what they were.

Officer Bill looked up as we closed the door. "Hi, Penny. Who's your friend?"

Sherlock was still wearing the wig and the dress. He pulled off the wig and pulled his own glasses out of his pocket.

Officer Bill's mouth actually dropped open. "Sherlock! What in the world?"

"Just a disguise," Sherlock said simply. "We're on a case."

Officer Bill stared at him, slowly shaking his head as if he couldn't quite believe what he was seeing. "I'm surprised that Watson here would want to be seen in public with you."

I wrinkled my nose at Officer Bill. "Watson?"

"Sure," Officer Bill grinned. "Remember Dr. Watson in the Sherlock Holmes series? He followed the detective around, helped somewhat in the investigations, and recorded the results. I figure what Dr. Watson was to Sherlock Holmes you are to Sherlock Jones here."

He looked Sherlock over with a very amused expression. "What have you been up to, dressed like that?"

"Just working on a case, sir." Sherlock was impatient to see the membership rolls from the labor union. He reached for the sheets in Chief Ramsey's hand, which were, of course, the object of his impatience. "Could I please have those, Chief?"

Officer Clark brushed him aside, as if he were a pesky gnat or mosquito. "Get lost, kid," he growled.

The chief looked from one officer to another. "Do either of you know what this is all about?" he asked. "Who sent this?"

Both men shook their heads. "I have no idea," Officer Bill replied.

"It came from the welders' union," the chief continued. He handed the papers to Clark. "Call over there and see what this is all about. Ask for Dan Griggs."

"No!" The word exploded from Sherlock's lips. "We just came from the welders' union. I had those papers sent! I need them for my investigation. Once I see those papers, I can tell you the name of the bank robber who shot Mr. Phillips."

He reached hopefully for the papers, but the tall officer jerked them out of reach. "Get lost, kid," he sneered. "We don't need your help with this investigation."

Officer Bill came to Sherlock's rescue. "What's this all about, Sherlock?"

"I sent the membership rolls from the welders' union," my friend explained. "Once I have them, I can give you the name and address of one of the robbers."

"How are you gonna do that, kid?" Officer Clark jeered, but Chief Ramsey cut him off.

"Give him the papers," he instructed the lieutenant. "Let's get back to work."

Clutching the precious papers, Sherlock and I hurried from the police station. "That was close," Sherlock commented. "If it had been up to Clark, we never would have gotten these."

We rode a block or two, and then Sherlock pulled into Waverly Park, pulled the papers from inside his dress, and began to examine them eagerly. "Nine pages," he said. "The receptionist must have changed her mind. She shut the machine down before it transmitted all the info."

"Maybe that Griggs character came in and told her to stop."

He looked crestfallen. "I just hope it includes the name we need."

He stuffed the pages back inside his dress and pedaled furiously for home. My breath was soon coming in ragged gasps as I struggled to keep up. As we turned into his driveway, Sherlock leaped from the rolling bicycle and dashed to his small office. The bike continued on its own accord and tore a jagged path through Mrs. Jones's flower bed. He didn't even notice.

I parked my bike in the proper fashion, removed Sherlock's bike from the marigolds, and hurried after him. Gravel crunched as a car turned into the driveway. I turned, and my heart sank when I saw a dark green Jaguar—Mrs. Rockwell.

The Jaguar purred to a stop, and the driver's window glided down noiselessly. Six or more large rings flashed in the sunlight as Mrs. Rockwell waved frantically in the direction of Sherlock's office. "Oh, Sherlock," she called from the open window, "I need your help, darling!"

Sherlock reappeared in the doorway of the little office with the sheaf of papers still in his hand. His face fell when he saw the

Jag, but he recovered quickly. He hurried forward with a polite smile on his face. "Mrs. Rockwell, how are you?" he said politely, but I could tell that he was anxious to examine the union rosters and was impatient at the delay.

Mrs. Rockwell is middle-aged, probably around thirty or thirty-two years old. Her husband owns a construction company in Spencerville, and they live in a humongous house between Willoughby and Spencerville. My dad says that Mr. Rockwell has more investments than I have freckles.

"Sherlock, darling, I need your help," the lady repeated.

"I'm afraid I can't right now, Mrs. Rockwell," my friend told her apologetically. "We're right in the middle of the bank robbery case. I'm trying to help Gimpy—"

"You two stay away from that Gimpy Williams character," Mrs. Rockwell warned us, looking from Sherlock to me. "That horrid man should still be in jail, after what he did! Why the police would ever release him is beyond me."

"Ma'am, there is a preponderance of evidence that proves that Gimpy was not involved in the robbery," Sherlock replied firmly. "That's the reason the Willoughby police released him."

She shook her head. "We all know better than that." She did her best to put on a helpless look. "Anyway, dear, will you help me?"

"I don't know that we can right now, Mrs. Rockwell."

"This is an emergency, darling! I'm scheduled to speak at the Rotary Club in Spencerville in about an hour, and I'm afraid it will be a disaster!"

She wrung her hands, and then looked at Sherlock. "Unless, of course, you can help me." I grimaced. Mrs. Rockwell always has to be so melodramatic.

Sherlock was impatient to get to the union roster, but he still was polite. He stifled a sigh. "At your service, Mrs. Rockwell. How may I help?"

Mrs. Rockwell let out a little moan, halfway between a whimper and a wail. "I've lost my glasses, darling. I won't be able to see my notes for my little speech at the Rotary, and there certainly isn't time to have another pair made. Whatever will I do?"

Sherlock sighed. "Where do you usually keep them?"

Our visitor patted a gold-colored handbag big enough to hold five copies of the New York City phone book. "They're always right here in my purse," she wailed, "but not now. And today of all days."

Sherlock glanced at the giant handbag. "You're certain they're not in there now?"

The woman nodded.

"When did you see them last?"

"I've been running errands all morning," she replied, "but I know I had them when I left the house."

"You're sure?"

Mrs. Rockwell nodded. "The mailman came just as I was leaving the house, so I pulled the car right up to the mailbox and went through the mail quickly. I can't read a thing without my glasses, so I know I had them then."

Sherlock frowned. "Do you use them to drive?"

Mrs. Rockwell shook her head. "They're reading glasses. I see just fine without them unless I'm reading or doing needle-point."

My friend folded his arms across his chest and pursed his lips thoughtfully. "You mentioned running errands. Where all did you go today?"

I was on pins and needles by now. Sherlock had the union roster in his hands, and here we were, discussing a missing pair of glasses! "Sherlock," I interrupted, "what about the fax we were going to look at? Did you forget it already?"

He waved a hand casually. "This'll just take a minute." He turned back to Mrs. Rockwell. "Tell me where you went this morning, and I'll try to figure out where the glasses are."

I snorted. Fat chance of finding Mrs. Rockwell's glasses, standing here in Sherlock's driveway! And the union names were first priority.

Mrs. Rockwell screwed up her face as she thought for a moment, then began to list the stops she had made, ticking off each place on her well-manicured fingertips. "Let's see now," she said, "I stopped by at our accountant's and picked up the payroll checks for my husband. Then I went by the fabric store and got some thread. I was halfway through a project, and I ran out of orange thread. Here, look."

She turned from the window of the car and picked up an item from the floorboard. She handed the object to Sherlock, and I saw that it was a beautiful butterfly, nearly finished, done in needlepoint. Glittering strands of fine orange and gold thread formed the butterfly's wings.

My friend handed the butterfly back. "It's beautiful! How did you pay for the thread?"

Mrs. Rockwell seemed insulted. "My dear young man, I am a woman of means," she snorted. "My husband owns—"

Sherlock patted her arm. "That's not what I mean," he interrupted. "How did you pay for your purchase? Cash? Check? Credit card?"

The wealthy woman relaxed. "I wrote a check. I was buying two pairs of Swiss-made scissors in addition to the thread."

Sherlock nodded. "I see. Where did you go from the fabric store?"

"I stopped for gas."

"Where?"

"We get our gas at the Parway distributor out on the highway," she answered. "My husband's company has an account there."

"Did you pay cash?"

"Oh, no," Mrs. Rockwell answered. "As I said, we have an account there. They just put it on the bill. I don't even have to sign for it."

I fidgeted nervously. *Come on, Sherlock!*

But Sherlock was in no hurry. "Where did you go next?" he queried.

"I made one more brief stop," Mrs. Rockwell answered. "I dropped some of my husband's blueprints off for Pete Groover to take a look at. He's an architect, you know."

Sherlock nodded. "I know. He has an office just down the street from the Willoughby bank. How were the blueprints packaged?" he asked. "Folded? Rolled up?"

"They were rolled up. In one of those long, cardboard mailing tubes."

"Did you open the tube?"

Mrs. Rockwell shook her head. "I was just dropping it off. I didn't even shut off the engine when I went in. And then I came here."

Sherlock looked puzzled. "Then when did you discover that your reading glasses were missing?"

"I was driving toward Spencerville," Mrs. Rockwell continued, "and I decided to look over my notes while I drove."

Sherlock really looked puzzled. "How can you see to drive with your reading glasses on?"

"Oh, I do it all the time," she answered brightly. "I just wear the glasses low on my nose. That way I can see through them to read, but I can still look over them from time to time to see the road."

Sherlock rolled his eyes. "Ma'am, if I may say so, that's not the safest way to drive."

Mrs. Rockwell shrugged. "It saves a lot of time."

Sherlock sighed deeply. "So you reached into your purse for your glasses, but they weren't there. So you turned around and came directly here, hoping I could help."

Mrs. Rockwell nodded. "You're my only hope, dear. I'm running late now, and my speech will be absolutely horrid if I can't read my notes!"

Sherlock leaned toward the car. "May I take a look into your purse, please?"

A shocked look flashed across the woman's face. She glanced at me, shrugged, and handed the monstrous object to my friend.

Sherlock opened it, glanced inside, and then closed it with a snap and handed it back. "Your glasses are at the fabric store, Mrs. Rockwell," he said simply. "On the counter."

I guess my mouth probably fell open as far as Mrs. Rockwell's did. She took the purse and then let out a little sigh as she dropped it on the car seat. "I really thought that you would help me, darling," she pouted, doing her best to let him see how disappointed she was.

"Your glasses are at the fabric store," Sherlock repeated, fishing a business card out of his pocket as he spoke. He handed it to her. "Do me a favor, would you? Call me from the fabric store when you find the glasses."

He glanced at me for the first time. "Now, if you'll excuse us, Penny and I are in the middle of a very important project."

We hurried into Sherlock's office as the Jaguar backed down the drive. "Well," I commented, "you finally got rid of her. I was afraid she was going to ask you to help her search for the glasses."

He looked at me reproachfully. "There was no need to search. We found them for her, didn't we?"

I snorted. "Found them? You have no idea where her glasses are any more than she does!"

Sherlock looked stunned and hurt. "Just wait for the phone call," he replied quietly.

He turned his attention to the newly acquired documents, placing the list of Keepsafe employees out on the plywood-and-cinder-block desk beside the union membership records, and then comparing the names on one list against the names on the other. I had never seen him so excited.

I sat down on the remaining milk crate and waited. He suddenly looked up with a grin, and I knew instantly that he had hit pay dirt. "Got it!" he cried triumphantly. "Michael Wilkinson, 113 Greenbriar Lane, Spencerville," he read from the page before him. "He's our man!"

Sherlock looked at me. "The fax machine apparently started with the last page and worked in reverse," he told me. "That's a good thing. If it had started with the *A*'s it would not have reached the *W*'s before the receptionist or Griggs or whoever turned it off."

He jumped to his feet. "I'll have a make on Wilkinson's car and license number in three minutes!" He dashed to the house, but I just sat and waited patiently.

Moments later, he scurried back with the phone line and the cordless phone, and hooked the line up to the modem on his computer. The phone rang suddenly, and he switched it on. "Sherlock here."

He listened for a moment, then replied, "Yes, Ma'am. Glad to help. Thanks for letting me know." He pushed a button to hang up.

"Who was that?" I asked.

He grinned. "Take a guess."

"Mrs. Rockwell."

He nodded. "Her glasses were on the counter at the fabric store, just as I told her."

I stared at him. "Then you weren't just guessing."

He frowned. "Of course not."

"Tell me how you knew," I begged. "It doesn't seem possible."

He shrugged. "It was simple. Mrs. Rockwell had the glasses when she left the house, since she was able to read the mail. But they weren't in her purse, or anywhere in the car, so I knew that she had left them at one of her stops."

"But she went to four different places," I protested. "How did you know which place she left them?"

"Penny, think!" he answered. "She had the glasses when she reached the fabric store, so we know she didn't leave them at the accountant's. That leaves only three possibilities."

"But how do you know she had them at the fabric store?" I countered.

"She needed them to be able to match the color of the thread," he answered, "and she wrote a check for her purchases. Both times she would have used her glasses. But at her last two stops—the gas pumps and the architect's—she didn't need her glasses. So where did she leave them? At the last place she used them, of course."

SHERLOCK JONES THE WILLOUGHBY BANK ROBBERY

I let out a sigh. It was all so easy, so logical. So why couldn't I learn to think that way?

He used his keyboard to dial a phone number from memory, explaining to me that he was accessing the DMV computers. In seconds, his printer began to click, and the information on Michael Wilkinson's vehicle appeared on the page.

When the machine was quiet again, Sherlock tore the page from the printer. "Look at this!" he shouted. "He's our man, all right! 1976 Chevrolet Impala, green, license number ARJ 551." He was so excited he actually did a little jig around the office.

"Let's go see Chief Ramsey!" he said, turning toward the door. I made it out the door ahead of him and scrambled onto my bike. I figured I needed as much of a head start as I could get.

When we reached the police station, I rushed in ahead of Sherlock. Chief Ramsey was alone in the office. "We found one of the bank robbers for you!" I blurted excitedly. "I mean, Sherlock found him. What I mean is, we haven't really found him for you, but we know who he is. Well, Sherlock does."

Sherlock gave me a funny look.

The chief looked skeptical as Sherlock gave him the name, address, and license number of the robber. "We'll check it out," he promised halfheartedly, turning to toss Sherlock's note casually onto a nearby desk.

I could tell that Sherlock was disappointed as we left police headquarters. "He didn't even believe me," he muttered, as we walked to our bikes. He was silent as we rode home, and I knew better than to bother him with my unanswered questions regarding the investigation.

That evening, Officer Bill came over to our house. "I called Sherlock and asked him to come over," he said mysteriously. "He'll be here in a few minutes. I thought you would want to come too." I tried and tried, but I couldn't get anything more out of him.

Moments after Officer Bill went home, Sherlock knocked on our door. We hurried over to Officer Bill's place. "What's this all about?" I asked, but Sherlock just shook his head.

"I have no idea," he answered. "But Officer Bill is certainly excited about something, isn't he?"

"Maybe they found the money from the bank robbery," I suggested.

Officer Bill greeted us with a huge grin, and I knew that something important had happened. As we plopped down on the couch in his living room, he tossed us each an icy cold can of soda pop. "Time to celebrate!" he said with a triumphant smile. "Thanks to Sherlock, we nailed one of the bank robbers. Michael Wilkinson of Spencerville."

Sherlock opened his drink and glanced up at Officer Bill. "I didn't think you guys were even gonna check it out," he replied.

The tall policeman nodded. "Chief Ramsey didn't think much of your information," he agreed, "but he and I went out to Greenbriar Lane to check it out. Wilkinson saw the squad car and tried to make a run for it. We arrested him, and Chief was convinced. He got a search warrant, and we found a long-barreled revolver identical to the one used in the robbery. We sent it to ballistics in Jackson, and they're working on it tonight. We should probably know tomorrow if it's the weapon that was used in the robbery."

The phone rang just then, and Officer Bill excused himself. I turned to Sherlock. "You were right," I congratulated him. "Wilkinson was one of the robbers. The police wouldn't have caught him without your help."

Sherlock just shrugged as if he had never had any doubt whatsoever that the investigation would turn out this way. I don't think he even considered the possibility that he could fail. But there was no pride or arrogance in his attitude; he simply expected to be successful.

Officer Bill entered the room just then. "That was Chief," he informed us. "Ballistics worked overtime, and they made a positive identification on the gun we found at Wilkinson's. The weapon matches the bullet that was taken from Mr. Phillips's chest. Wilkinson will be charged with armed robbery, assault with a deadly weapon, and attempted murder. And thanks to Sherlock, we'll have a pretty good case against him."

"Then the case is solved," I said to Sherlock. "Congratulations!"

He shook his head. "We still don't have the other gunman," he replied.

Officer Bill nodded, agreeing with Sherlock. "We didn't find the money from the bank either," he mentioned. "It wasn't at Wilkinson's house. They nearly tore his place apart looking for it. Somewhere out there is $180,000—in cash."

TEN

A TRAGIC RESULT

The knock at the door was unexpected, and it startled all three of us. Officer Bill went to answer it. When he came back into the room he was followed by Gimpy Williams.

"I just came by to tell you all goodbye," Gimpy said softly.

I sprang to my feet. "Goodbye?" I echoed. "Where are you going?"

Gimpy looked at the floor. "I put my property up for sale today. I'm moving up near Chicago where my sister lives. She and her husband have agreed to put me up for awhile until I decide what I'm going to do and where I'm going to live."

I grabbed his arm. "Gimpy! Why leave Willoughby? You've lived here all your life!"

He nodded sadly. "I know. But I can't stay in Willoughby any longer. Not after what happened."

"But your name has been cleared," Sherlock argued, rising from the couch to approach us. "Leave this thing behind you and move on. It's over."

Gimpy shook his head. "I can't, Sherlock."

"Why not?" The question came from Officer Bill.

"I guess you might say that I found out who my friends are," the man answered slowly. "Except for the three of you, it looks like I just don't have any friends in Willoughby. When you think about it, there's no reason to stay, is there?"

"Now, that's not really true," I told him. "You have lots of friends here."

He laughed bitterly. "Sure I do, Penny." He held up one hand and began to count off on his fingertips with the other hand. "There's the Portlocks and the Andersons and Mrs. Smedley and . . ."

"OK," I told him, "there were people who were against you, and some who even told you so. But not everybody was against you. You know that!"

He turned to me, and I saw the deep pain reflected in his eyes. "Penny, do you know how many people came up to me and said a kind word? Not one! No one came and said 'Gimpy, we know you didn't do it.' Or, 'Gimpy, we're praying for you.' Not one."

His shoulders sagged as he spoke. "Even after I was cleared and that other feller was arrested, not one person told me they were sorry that I went through what I did."

I hurt inside for him. "I'm so sorry," I whispered.

"The worst part was that my brothers and sisters in the Lord treated me the same way as the unsaved folks did," he continued. "I thought they would understand, that they would stand with me, that they would pray for me. But no, they talked about me just as much as anybody!"

He sighed. "That was the hardest part."

Officer Bill, Sherlock and I stood silent for several long, tense seconds. Finally, Sherlock spoke. "It wasn't the Lord Who abandoned you, Gimpy."

"Oh, I know that," the big man said quickly. "I ain't blamin' the Lord one bit, no siree. But I am kinda disappointed in some of His people."

"We're sorry this happened, Gimpy," Officer Bill said quietly.

Gimpy nodded. "Now what I just said doesn't go for you three, OK? You three stood with me, and I'm grateful. It's the rest of this town that I'm talking about."

"What are you going to do?" Sherlock asked. "You aren't going to turn your back . . ." He paused.

"On the Lord?" Gimpy finished for him. "Now, Sherlock, you know me better than that! I'm eternally grateful to the Lord Jesus, and I'll stay faithful to Him. He's never let me down, and I ain't about to let Him down. I'll find me a good, Bible-preaching church somewhere and keep serving the Lord. But I just can't do it in Willoughby."

He looked from Sherlock to Officer Bill to me. "Well, this is it, I guess. I want to thank you three for believin' in me, even if no one else did. Goodbye, and keep me in your prayers."

Without another word, he turned and slipped out into the night.

Sherlock walked over and sat on the couch with a long sigh. I dropped to a seat on the other end. Officer Bill stood looking out the window into the darkness of the evening. No one said a word for several minutes.

"If only someone in this town had used his tongue for encouragement," Sherlock said softly, "instead of using it to tear down and criticize."

"These people were so sure they knew what had happened," Officer Bill said angrily. "They were quick to judge and gossip, but even after the truth came out, no one was willing to go to Gimpy and try to set things right, try to help restore him."

"You were right," I told Sherlock. "On the day of the robbery you said that someone would get hurt when the rumors started flying. Gimpy got hurt, and now he's leaving Willoughby for good. He'll carry this hurt for the rest of his life."

He nodded. "We have a responsibility to use our tongues correctly." He sighed. "I just wish that I had realized what Gimpy was going through and tried to be an encouragement to him."

"You never sided with those who were sure he was guilty," I argued, "and you did clear his name."

"Sure, I stood with him in that way," Sherlock replied. "I knew he wasn't guilty, and I did my best to clear his name, but I didn't go to him and actually encourage him—tell him that I was praying for him and that the Lord would see him through this. I just wish that I had done that. I wasn't sensitive to what Gimpy was feeling."

"I think we can all learn a lesson from this," Officer Bill said, smiling sadly. "Perhaps all of Willoughby can . . . or at least the believers."

"Next time it will be different for me," I vowed. "I'm asking the Lord to help me to always use my tongue to encourage others."

And I meant it.

ELEVEN

A SECRET MESSAGE

Willoughby may be a small town, but we do have our own newspaper. It comes out once a week, usually on Wednesday. Several days had passed since the arrest of Michael Wilkinson, and the next issue of the Willoughby Gazette carried the story of the robbery and detailed the arrest of Wilkinson.

I was furious when I finished the article. It told of the video-tape from the security camera at the bank and how the subsequent investigation led to Wilkinson. There was one major problem with the article. It didn't even mention Sherlock.

I gritted my teeth in frustration as I read.

One of the alleged gunmen involved in last week's armed robbery of the First National Bank of Willoughby was arrested at his home this week by Willoughby police officers. Michael David Wilkinson of Spencerville was charged with armed robbery, assault with a deadly weapon, and attempted murder. Judge Larson will set a date for a hearing later this month.

The police force of Willoughby is to be commended for its fine detective work and painstaking attention to detail its investigation of this case. Lieutenant Clark, who led the investigation, is an exceptional officer, and much of the credit for the success of the investigation is rightfully his.

Officer Clark, we commend you for a job well done.

The article concluded with a report on the progress of Mr. Phillips. It stated that he would be released from General Hospital shortly.

I biked over to Sherlock's just to show him the article. He read it and then shrugged as he handed the paper back to me. "That's the way it is," he said, nonchalantly. "One person does the work, another gets the credit. What's new?"

"But doesn't that bug you?" I insisted. "They didn't even mention you in the article!"

"That's the way it is, Penny," he said again. "But it really doesn't matter. As Christians, we are supposed to have servants' hearts. A servant doesn't worry about whether or not he gets the credit for his actions. His desire is to bring honor to his Master."

I pedaled home, and I was still angry as I parked my bike in the garage. It wasn't fair! The only thing that pompous Lieutenant Clark had done was laugh at Sherlock when he presented his clues. Then the *Gazette* gives Clark the credit, as if he were responsible for Wilkinson's arrest! It might not matter to Sherlock, but it sure bugged me.

The $180,000 from the robbery was still missing. Mike Wilkinson wasn't talking. He refused to name his accomplice, and he wouldn't even discuss the whereabouts of the stolen money. The police were at a standstill.

Several evenings later, Sherlock and I went over to Officer Bill's just to discuss the robbery and the missing loot. Officer Bill acted as if he were tired of the whole matter.

"We're getting nowhere," he fumed. "Wilkinson isn't talking, and we have no idea who his buddy was or what they did with the money."

He drew a paper from his pocket, unfolded it, and handed it to Sherlock. "See what you can make of this," he requested. "Wilkinson tried to sneak it out of jail via Larry Adams, the custodian at the county jail. Adams turned it over to us."

Sherlock glanced at the paper. "It's a photocopy."

Officer Bill nodded. "Chief Ramsey has the original note. He's sending it to the FBI tomorrow. We couldn't make anything of it."

"What did Wilkinson want Adams to do with it?" Sherlock asked.

"He was to leave it in the bushes beside the roadside rest area on Highway 65," Officer Bill answered. "Tomorrow he was to pick up an answer in the same place, along with payment for his services as courier."

"Be sure to stake out the rest area," the boy detective suggested.

Officer Bill nodded. "We already have," he answered. "Two officers from Jackson are out there now. Chief Ramsey figured that the other gunman might get suspicious if two Willoughby officers disappeared from circulation."

Sherlock turned his attention to the sheet of paper in his hand. I slipped over beside him and looked over his shoulder. It was easy, since he is so much shorter than I am.

The message didn't make any sense. Here's all it said:

WHISTLE FKKQ BP HROBTS E'P MFWIT 220 YWOSP
TWPQ KL HWID SKKO RJSTO QWFF PMORIT GKUT QK
WFQTOJWQT FKIWQBKJ OTMFY PWGT.

I looked from Sherlock to Officer Bill. "It doesn't make any sense at all!" I declared "The only word written in English is 'whistle.'"

"It's in cipher," Sherlock told me.

"What?"

"Cipher," he repeated. "It's a secret code. Each letter in the code stands for another letter."

Officer Bill nodded. "We figured that much," he agreed. "But none of us have had much experience with cipher, and we can't figure this one out for anything. The FBI boys will have this tomorrow, and they'll know what to do with it. But they move so slowly, it'll probably be several days before they get to it."

"Let's solve it tonight," I suggested. "Please, Sherlock?"

He looked apathetic. "I guess we could," he conceded.

"How would we do it?" Officer Bill asked.

"There are several different ways," Sherlock explained. "One is to notice the frequency of letter usage, and figure out bits of the message from that, until the whole makes sense. For instance, in the English language, *e* is the most frequently used letter. After it come *t* and *a,* followed by *o, n, i, r, s,* and *h,* which occur about equally often, and tapering down to the rare ones like *j, k, q, x,* and *z.*"

He glanced back at the paper. "But this message is really too short for that. There's a much easier way. This is a key word cipher; in fact, the key word is given right here: *whistle.*"

"What does that mean?" I asked.

"I'll show you," he replied. "In fact, you can be the one to decipher the message." He turned to Officer Bill. "Get Penny a sheet of paper and a pencil, will you?"

I sat down at Officer Bill's kitchen table with the pencil in hand. "What do I do?"

"Start with your key word," the boy detective instructed. "Write it across the top of the page, over to the left."

I wrote W-H-I-S-T-L-E in capital letters.

"Now write the alphabet on the same line beside it," Sherlock told me, "but leave out the letters in the word 'whistle.'"

When I finished, the first line on my paper looked like this:

W H I S T L E A B C D F G J K M N O P Q R U V X Y Z

"Now write the entire alphabet directly below the key line."

I stared at him blankly. "Huh?"

"Put an *a* below the *w*, a *b* below the *h*, a *c* below the *i*," he explained patiently. "When the entire alphabet is written, you can decipher the message."

Finally, I understood, and followed his instructions. When I had finished, my page now looked like this:

W H I S T L E A B C D F G J K M N O P Q R U V X Y Z
A B C D E F G H I J K L M N O P Q R S T U V W X Y Z

"The rest is easy," Sherlock said. "This is a very simple cipher. To solve it, simply find the enciphered letters one by one in the key line, and then read the letter directly below. Write each letter above the cipher letter in the message."

I caught on and began to decipher the message. Sherlock was right. It was easy, once I knew what to do. The first line of the message,

FKKQ BP HROBTS E'P MFWIT

Now looked like this—

LOOT IS BURIED G'S PLACE
FKKQ BP HROBTS E'P MFWIT

Officer Bill gave a low whistle and said, "Well, what do you know? We sweated over this message for hours and got absolutely nowhere. It's embarrassing to think that it was this easy!"

He chuckled. "Sherlock, please don't tell anyone how you showed us up today, OK?"

Sherlock laughed and shrugged. "Fine with me."

I continued to work on the cipher, and when I had finished, the entire message read:

LOOT IS BURIED G'S PLACE 220 YARDS EAST OF BACK DOOR UNDER TALL SPRUCE MOVE TO ALTERNATE LOCATION REPLY SAME

All three of us stared at it in silence. "What does it mean?" I asked.

Sherlock spoke up. "The $180,000 is buried at G's place," he explained, "under a tall spruce 220 yards east of G's back door. Wilkinson wants his partner to move the loot to another location, and send him a reply by the same method."

He frowned. "If we knew who *G* is, we would know where the money is."

I laughed out loud as a sudden thought occurred to me. "I know who it is!" I shouted.

Officer Bill and Sherlock instantly turned toward me. "You do?" they chorused together.

"Yes," I declared. "*G* has to be short for 'Gimpy!'"

Sherlock slapped his forehead. "Of course. I should have thought of that! The money is buried in the woods behind Gimpy's house!" He looked at me. "Thanks, Watson."

I was pleased that at least I had figured something out before Sherlock had. I knew it would be a long time before I had a chance to do that again.

Officer Bill jumped up and hurried from the room. When he returned, he was carrying a shovel and two flashlights. I noticed that his service revolver was strapped on his hip. "How would you two like to run a little errand with me?" he asked. "You can help me dig up over a sixth of a million dollars in cash! Might as well do it tonight—before Gimpy finds out just how much his property is worth."

I sat in front between Officer Bill and Sherlock as we drove out toward Gimpy's. Sherlock leaned over and whispered, "I just thought of a way to make Wilkinson name his accomplice. We'll work on it tomorrow morning."

Several minutes later, Officer Bill turned the car into the driveway leading to Gimpy's house. He shut off the lights and cruised quietly down the narrow lane. When we were about a hundred yards from the house, he gently braked to a stop. We quietly got out and slipped around behind the silent house.

While Sherlock and I watched, Officer Bill quietly walked to Gimpy's back door and then carefully began to step off two hundred twenty yards due east. We followed him into the dark woods.

TWELVE

SHERLOCK SETS A TRAP

The next morning, Sherlock and I watched as Officer Bill stacked bundle after bundle of tens and twenties on the police dispatcher's desk. I enjoyed the look of astonishment on the faces of Chief Ramsey and Lieutenant Clark. $180,000 makes quite an impressive pile.

Mr. Gillis was there as well as a bank examiner. The money was to be returned to the bank vault under the protective presence of Officer Bill and Officer Clark.

This time Officer Bill gave Sherlock full credit for the success of the investigation from the arrest of Wilkinson to the recovery of the missing money. Mr. Gillis was amazed at the shrewd reasoning of the young detective. As Officer Bill finished his narrative, Clark stood by sullenly with a look of jealousy creasing his sharp features.

"All we need now is the identity of the other suspect," Chief Ramsey commented. He turned to Sherlock. "Young man," he said with a slight smile, "you've proved your competence as a detective. You're amazing, especially for someone so young! Think you can help us find the other gunman?"

Sherlock nodded. "Yes, sir," he replied, "I've thought of a way—"

Chief Ramsey had already turned back to Officer Bill. "Our boys at the rest area stakeout came within a hair of nabbing the other suspect. Adams left a dummy package in the bushes early this morning, and within half an hour, we had a customer. When the officers moved in, however, he got away through the woods. We had expected him to come by car, not on foot. We're dealing with a sharp operator."

"You can forget the stakeout now," Sherlock suggested.

The chief nodded. "He won't come back to the drop point now. And Wilkinson still isn't talking. Unless he breaks, we'll never identify the second robber."

"I think I can help you with that," the boy detective said. He pulled a folded paper from his pocket. "Have Adams slip this to Wilkinson, as if it's a reply to his message. When he reads it, I think he'll talk."

Chief Ramsey unfolded Sherlock's note and spread it on the desk for all to see. I crowded close in with everyone else, but the note was in cipher. Here's what it said:

JAILHOUSE RSJGCQ OKP RSH EGOK, MJPRGHP.
E'F FKVEGU RSH DKKR—RK JGKRSHP QRJRH.
QK DKGU, QTICHP.
YKT CGKW WSK

I looked at Sherlock. "What does it say?"

He just grinned at me. "You know how to do ciphers now. Figure it out."

I began to copy the enciphered note, and he turned to Chief Ramsey. "Will you have Adams deliver it to Wilkinson's cell," he asked, "as if it's a reply to the original message? Once Wilkinson deciphers it, I think he'll be ready to name his accomplice in the bank robbery."

When I was finished copying, the chief folded the note and handed it to Officer Bill. "I guess it's worth a try," he answered Sherlock. "Officer Bill, have Adams get this to Wilkinson."

He turned back to the young detective. "Thanks, Sherlock."

While Mom was preparing lunch, I spread my copy of the note on the kitchen table and began to decipher it. I wrote the word JAILHOUSE at the top of a new page, then the rest of the alphabet beside it. Then I wrote the entire alphabet below that line. Mom got interested in what I was doing and forgot all about lunch. She looked over my shoulder and saw:

J A I L H O U S E B C D F G K M N P Q R T V W X Y Z
A B C D E F G H I J K L M N O P Q R S T U V W X Y Z

I explained the cipher system to her as I worked on Sherlock's note, and she caught on quickly. (My mom is smart!) She helped with the deciphering on the last couple lines of the note. When we had finished, we read:

> *THANKS FOR THE INFO, PARTNER.*
> *I'M MOVING THE LOOT—TO ANOTHER STATE.*
> *SO LONG, SUCKER.*
> *YOU KNOW WHO*

Mom and I looked at each other. "Wow!" I said, as I realized what Sherlock was trying to do. "When Wilkinson deciphers this, he'll be furious! At least, if he really thinks it came from his partner in the robbery."

Mom laughed. "That friend of yours is a character, isn't he? We'll have to wait and see if Wilkinson takes the bait."

That evening, Sherlock and I were in my front yard catching fireflies when we saw Officer Bill drive in. He parked and sauntered over to see us. I could tell he had some news for us and was just about to burst if he couldn't tell it.

"You did it, buddy!" he called to Sherlock. "Wilkinson walked right into your trap! He named his accomplice in the robbery! We arrested the second gunman just about an hour ago."

"Who was it?" Sherlock asked, and I glanced at him in surprise. Somehow, it just hadn't occurred to me that he really didn't know. I mean, it seems like he always knows everything.

"His partner was Griggs," Officer Bill answered, "the rep from the welders' union. Wilkinson spilled his guts and told us the whole story. Griggs is a compulsive gambler and had taken nearly fifty thousand dollars from union retirement funds. You guessed it: he lost it all at the tables. An auditor that the union hired was getting close to discovering the missing funds, and that's when Griggs teamed up with Wilkinson to pull off the bank job.

"When Wilkinson deciphered your note, he was furious. He was determined to nail Griggs, thinking that Griggs was trying to take off with the loot and leave him with the rap for the bank robbery. He called for Chief Ramsey and talked his head off. He said enough to put both of them behind bars for quite a while."

"What would you have done," I asked Sherlock, "if Wilkinson hadn't fallen for your trap?"

"There was another way to find out the identity of the second gunman," he replied, "but I didn't want to use it unless I had to. It was more fun this way."

"You are one smart kid!" Officer Bill exclaimed. "I still can't believe you solved this whole thing by yourself!"

"I didn't," Sherlock replied. "The Lord was with me. I asked for His help constantly throughout this whole investigation."

"Mr. Gillis told us there's a reward coming from the bank," Officer Bill went on. "As far as I can see, it's all yours."

Sherlock glanced at me. "Watson here helped too," he said. "She deserves half the reward."

And that's what happened. Several days later, Mr. Gillis presented Sherlock and me each with a check for a thousand dollars! Our pictures were in the paper and everything! After I tithed on my reward money, I put the rest in the bank, so now I have nine hundred and thirty-nine dollars in my account. You can figure out for yourself how much Sherlock has.

But anyway, back to our conversation with Officer Bill and Sherlock in the front yard. After Officer Bill told us about the bank reward, he turned back to Sherlock. "There's something I've been wanting to ask you, Mr. Hotshot Detective," he said. "How in the world did you know to go to Keepsafe armored securities and the welders' union for clues? How did you know that Wilkinson had worked for Keepsafe and that he was a welder?"

I had been wondering the same thing myself, but Sherlock had never told me. But now that Officer Bill had asked, he seemed ready to divulge his secrets.

"Mr. Gillis told Penny and me that the robbery seemed to be an inside job," Sherlock replied. "But he was positive that neither of the robbers had ever worked for the bank! That left only one other possibility: one or both of the robbers had worked for the armored truck agency and had made deliveries to the bank."

"How did you know that one of the robbers was a welder?" I asked.

"I can show you better than tell you," he answered. He looked back at the tall policeman. "Officer Bill, do you still have access to that videotape from the robbery?"

Officer Bill nodded. "I've got a copy at my house now," he replied. "But I don't see what that has to do with Wilkinson being a welder."

"Run the tape, and I'll show you," Sherlock offered.

Moments later, we were seated in front of Officer Bill's TV. He popped a tape into the VCR and then handed the remote control to Sherlock. Suddenly we were watching the now familiar film of the Willoughby bank robbery. The robbers walked across the screen toward the camera. The man in front, the one with the shotgun, stepped out of the picture, and for just an instant, the image of the man with the revolver filled the screen. At that instant, Sherlock put the tape on pause.

"Look at his arms," he instructed, and Officer Bill and I both crowded close to the screen. "What do you see?"

"He's wearing short sleeves," I ventured.

"Yes, but what else?" Sherlock prodded.

Officer Bill and I shrugged. Sherlock touched the screen. "Look closely," he instructed. "His arms are covered with small scars."

I leaned forward intently, and sure enough, now that Sherlock had pointed them out, I could see the scars were there.

"Those are burns," he told us. "Notice that he has them on both arms. His forearms have a number of small scars from burns, but look at this—they stop about six inches from his wrists. There are no burns anywhere near his hands. What does that tell you?"

"He was wearing gloves when he was burned," Officer Bill answered.

"Right," Sherlock returned. "His hands were always protected by leather gloves—welders' gloves. This is not a right-to-work-state, so I figured if he's a welder, he's got to be a union member. We had figured that he lived in this area, and I could tell from his arms that he had been welding recently, so I figured we would find his name on the local welders' union rolls.

"Once we had the union membership lists, all I had to do was compare the names with those on the Keepsafe employee lists, and the name that appeared on both lists was our man! Wilkinson was the only welder who had also worked for Keepsafe."

Officer Bill laughed. "So simple," he said, "and yet we couldn't see it. Sherlock, you've outdone the entire Willoughby police force. All three of us!"

We laughed as Officer Bill poured each of us a soft drink.

"The Lord was good to us," Sherlock said softly, "and guided us in each step of the investigation. There were several times when this whole thing could have gone wrong, and the Lord worked it out perfectly each time. We have to be careful to give Him the credit; we dare not take it ourselves."

I thought back over the fast-paced events of the last few days, remembering the lady tourist with the camera, the shock of coming face to face with the armed gunmen, and the excitement of watching Sherlock unravel the clues of the case so effortlessly.

"I wish that Gimpy hadn't left town," I said wistfully, "but I'm glad that the whole thing's over."